The O'Brien

A Ballysea Mystery

Frances Powell

This is a work of fiction. Names, characters,
places and incidents either are products of the
author's imagination or are used fictitiously.
Any resemblance to actual events, locales or
persons, living or dead, is entirely
coincidental.

Cover by: Jo Stallings

ISBN 9 7 8 - 1 - 4 8 3 5 6 - 2 1 4 - 8

This book is dedicated to my daughter Michele
who never stopped believing in me.

To Mark,
Best wishes/
Tron Powell

Chapter 1

She must have come in the night because the first that anyone saw of her was in the wee hours of the breaking day. But as the sun came up and began to reflect across the sea, the villagers were already buzzing about the lady and the beast that walked along the shore.

Mary McIntyre was the first to see her or so she said, but then again Mary was always the first to see everything in Ballysea. Rising from bed before the dawn of day came naturally for Mary after more than 30 years of rising from her bed at 3:00 am to prepare breakfast for her fisherman husband and bake the loaves of bread she sold at the village market. Mary had long continued the habit even after the market and her husband had both gone to dust.

"You should have seen her," she whispered. Mary had a way of telling a story and she knew that whispering would draw her audience closer into the web of mystery her story would soon weave. "Her hair, it was sparkling in the sun, like the veins of gold that run through the mines and that beast beside her, he came neigh up to her chest. I have never seen one the size and likes of him but pretty as you please with his lady. The minute that she tarried, he sat and waited, and never made a move even when old Maggie Connolly's cat ran right across his path. It was as if he had never seen it. It is that well behaved the big beastie is. And dressed lovely she was, with the softest of blue shawl about her shoulders and down her back."

"Slow down now Mary. Did you see where she went or know who she might be visiting?" asked Mr. O'Dougle, the green grocer.

"I was getting to that if you will just give me but a second."

Pausing for just a few seconds to get the full effect, she pointed her arthritic deformed finger and whispered," she went into the old O'Bannon Croft."

"Are you sure then, Mary? That place has been empty for nearly a year now," said O'Dougle as he scratched his head and peered out the window toward the house at the far end of the village.

"Of course, I am sure. Didn't I see her and the beastie with my own two eyes open that very door and go in and shut it behind her? Used a key she did, so she must be owning it or so I would think."

"Well, if she does then I guess I will be meeting her soon enough being the only grocer in town. She'll have to come in here soon enough to buy a few bits and pieces and god knows we can all use a little more business. Pity I'm not the butcher, because the way Mary describes that dog I'll wager he takes a lot of feeding!" laughed O'Dougle.

"Just watch how you be treating the lady, O'Dougle, or that beastie may decide you look like a good meal," snickered Mary as she tapped his rounded belly with the handle of her umbrella and walked out the door.

The walk on the beach had helped clear the cobwebs from Catherine's head and the fresh brewed pot of coffee would surely finish the job.

The flight and the long drive to the remote seaside village had left her drained. The estate agent was kind enough to leave a basket of necessities and a bucket of coal to get her through her first two days, as well as seen to it that the house had been swept fairly clean and fresh linens placed on the bed and in the bath. With the furniture lorry not due to arrive with her household goods for another two weeks she was going to have to make the best of what she managed to carry in her two large suitcases and make do with the furniture that was left in the house when her friend's aunt passed away last year.

Catherine wandered over to the ancient refrigerator and pulling open the door was delighted to find a bottle of milk, butter and some lovely white cheddar. Giggling like a schoolgirl, she pulled out the bounty and ceremoniously spread it on the large weathered farmhouse table and declared, "Look O'Brien, we are going to have a feast! I'm really going to have to send some flowers to that estate agent!"

O'Brien arose from his resting place on the tattered rag rug in front of the open fireplace and stretching out slowly walked up to the table until his chin rested even with the cheese that had been placed there.

"Oh no, you don't, O'Brien. Don't you be starting any new bad habits here. We both know you are quite tall enough to stand up and eat off the table with me and not that it would bother me but I think we should not be learning any new habits that might upset our new neighbors. I am sure that the look of you has them talking enough!" laughed Cat as she gently stoked the head of her gentle protector.

Slicing off a thick piece of the grain bread for her and one for O'Brien, she spread them with sweet butter and topped them with the cheddar. Pouring a steaming cup of coffee, she settled down and trading bite for bite with O'Brien soon finished off their breakfast. Now there was nothing left but to have her second cup of coffee and her morning cigarette before clearing up the dishes. Her smoking habit was something that Cat had never quite managed to defeat. Although she had managed to control it and limit it to one after every meal and one at bedtime with a glass of wine, she rationalized that she had come a long way from that pack a day habit not that long ago.

Wandering around the one room that was to serve as her kitchen, dining room and sitting room, Cat began to visualize how she would place her furniture and other belongings once they arrived. There was much to do within the next two weeks and she reckoned the hard work would be just the therapy she needed to get herself prepared to start rebuilding her life. Sitting down at the table, she stretched out her long legs and watched the steam from the coffee and the smoke from the cigarette filter about the small room. 'Yellow', she thought. 'That's it. The room needs to be sunshine yellow. That will go well with my blue and white sofas and chairs. White trim on the woodwork will brighten the room and lace curtains at the window will give me all the light and privacy I will need.' Cat was beginning to picture how it would all come together as she leaned her head back and took a final drag from her cigarette and

8

exhaled. She was getting excited now and was ready to get on with the work!

"Before we set about cleaning this place and getting it ready for a new coat of paint, we best walk into town and get some provisions for the next couple of days. Come along O'Brien. We might as well let the good town folk get a close up look at the two of us."

Opening the door and stepping out into the crisp late spring air, Cat took a deep breath and smelled the scent of the sea mixed with the lavender in the remains of the small now over-grown cottage garden. The cottage itself was a traditional Irish croft made of local stone with one large room taking up the entire ground floor. The kitchen and dining area took up one half of the room and the cozy parlor the other. Cat couldn't help but think to herself that the Irish had been centuries ahead of the Americans when it came to open concept living. Upstairs was a carbon copy of the ground floor and provided her sleeping quarters including a large, lovely but dated bath that had obviously been added within the last ten years to replace the outhouse. 'Thank goodness for that,' thought Cat!

"Soon as we get the inside cleaned, we have to sort out this poor garden. I can't abide dead things at my doorway." Little did she think that these words would soon come back to haunt her.

With O'Brien by her side she wandered slowly down the narrow lane that separated her cottage from the beach below and past the small nearly deserted harbor into town. As she passed each brightly painted storefront she stopped to look in each of the shop windows and make a mental note of where she might want to come to purchase the items she would need over the next few weeks to get her new home ready. As she walked, she tried to imagine what the fishing village must have looked like in better days when the harbor had been bustling with boats of all sizes laden with their bounty from the sea. She could see the remains of what appeared to have been a good sized market house where she pictured the people from the surrounding area selling all sorts of produce and wares.

When she stopped to look at the fruits and vegetables on offer outside of the Green Grocer, Mr. O'Dougle, the proprietor of the small but well stocked store, came from behind the counter to open the door and welcome her into his shop. "Hello, you must be the new lady at the Croft and this must be himself that we have all heard about. Welcome to Ballysea. I'm John O'Dougle and it is nice to make your acquaintance," said the green grocer as he wiped his hands on his large white apron before extending them to Cat.

"Catherine Murphy and himself is The O'Brien but if he likes you well enough you can get by with just O'Brien," smiled Cat as she reached for the grocer's large calloused outstretched hand. "We'll be needing some potatoes, onions and carrots please and some apples as well."

"You just pick out what you need and I'll bag and weigh it over here for you."

As Mr. O'Dougle was weighing up her purchases, Cat took the time to wander the spotlessly clean shop and stopping at a counter laden with large round loaves of crusty bread with a cross in the middle she exclaimed, "My goodness, this looks just like the bread my granny used to bake."

"Ah, then your granny must have been Irish because those are soda breads," replied the grocer as he finished bagging her produce.

"Indeed she was. Both my grandparents were born and raised in Sligo but moved to America right after they were married. I'll have a loaf of the white please and could you tell me where there might be a good butcher?"

"We only have one in town and whether he is good or not is anyone's guess but we don't have much choice around here. He's right down the lane here on the left side of the road," said the grocer as he pointed out the window.

"Would you like me to hold onto your purchases until you come back up this way? Then you won't have to carry your parcels through the whole village."

"That would be very kind of you, Mr. O'Dougle," replied Cat as she paid for her purchases. "I shouldn't be long. Come along O'Brien, you can pick out your own dinner tonight."

O'Dougle observed that the giant of a dog had not moved a hair since his mistress had crossed the threshold into his shop, but the beasts alert gray eyes never left her. He seemed to be constantly on the guard protecting his lady. O'Dougle reckoned he was the biggest of his breed that he had ever seen. He remembered when there used to be a lot of them about in the old days, especially around the old estates but now a day people preferred the smaller breeds that took up less room and ate less too. Yes, O'Dougle reckoned that The O'Brien was the most impressive Irish Wolfhound he had ever seen.

O'Brien slowly rose to his feet and slipped his big head under his mistress's hand as they walked through the village. The sea of morning shoppers seem to part as The O'Brien guided his mistress down the narrow lane toward the butcher. Catherine smiled and greeted all those she passed but all eyes were on her companion as his sheer size stole the show.

13

"Now isn't that a sight," murmured O'Dougle as a smile spread across his weathered face.

Crossing the street to the butcher, The O'Brien positioned himself in front of the display window laden with fresh cuts of beef and lamb and poultry of every description.

"So, what shall it be tonight my handsome lad?" whispered Cat to O'Brien as she gently stroked his head.

As if he understood every word that she said, his eyes moved back and forth across the window and stopped and rested on the large roasting chicken. As his tail began to wag excitedly Cat said, "So, it's a roast chicken dinner for tonight, eh? Well, good choice my lad, with the size of that one we will have our lunch for tomorrow too. Now, you wait right here and I'll go collect our dinner."

Cat entered the shop and quietly waited for her turn. The butcher, James Burke seemed a serious sort. He neither introduced himself nor made any attempt to find out anything about the

14

stranger. He merely took her order and went to the window to retrieve the chicken. It must have been then that he spotted The O'Brien for the first time.

"For the love of god, have you ever seen such a big fellow in your life? I thought I was seeing things!" exclaimed Mr. Burke excitedly.

"Oh, I' m sorry if he startled you. He's my companion and he's just waiting for me to finish my shopping," spoke Cat softly.

"Oh, he didn't startle me. More just surprised me. I haven't seen one so bonny in years. You see, my grandfather had a wolfhound and I loved that dog. He was my best playmate growing up and a better friend a child never had," replied James Burke as a smile spread across his face as he thought of the calmer and happier days of his youth.

"I am terribly sorry. I must apologize for my rudeness. My name is James Burke and you must be the new owner of the Croft. I heard from the estate agent you might be arriving soon."

Cat took the outstretched hand of the butcher and introducing herself smiled and thought how often her big friend had made introductions much easier.

"May I offer him a treat?"

"If it would please you. I am sure that The O'Brien won't complain," smiled Cat warmly. Cat's gaze met O'Brien's and with one movement of her hand to her side, the big dog moved quickly through the doorway and sat on the sawdust covered floor by her side.

"It is best if I introduce you first so that he will know that it is alright to accept food from you. O'Brien, please shake hands with Mr. Burke."

The O'Brien raised his left paw and placed it firmly in the outstretched right hand of the butcher and stared into his face.

"Ah ha, he is searching my face for signs of deceit," said Mr. Burke with a smile as he shook the offered paw. "My grandfather's hound did the very same thing. Grandfather said that they were gifted at reading what was in a man's soul by just gazing into his eyes."

"Now, would you like a treat?" he asked.

The O'Brien's head began to bob up and down in a nodding manner as Mr. Burke chuckled and reached for a large cube of beef.

"I could swear that he understood exactly what I just said," laughed Mr. Burke as he handed over the treat to his new found friend.

"Well, there's a good lad. You be sure to bring him when you come again, I've always got treats for the likes of him."

Cat smiled brightly at Mr. Burke as they finished the exchange and upon leaving the shop was surprised to see a group of towns' people staring in through the window.

"Oh dear, I am afraid I have been keeping business from you", sighed Cat as she left the shop waving goodbye to the butcher.

"Good morning," she said to the curious on lookers. Touching O'Brien's head with her hand,

"I hope my companion hasn't given you cause for fright."

They all looked at her with confused expressions until one elderly lady whispered, "No miss, it's not the beastie, but Mr. Burke, the butcher. You see, he hasn't even smiled since his daughter drowned out there in the bay some years back. The sea took her. Not even a body to visit in the churchyard. When we heard him laughing just now, we were afraid that the poor man had finally lost his mind completely. It is a miracle that big dog has done."

Cat hesitated for a minute, before replying. "I don't know about performing miracles but The O'Brien does seem to have a special understanding of people in need."

Chapter 2

Walking back through the village towards the green grocers and home, she thought about the first time she met The O'Brien.

No one could have been more in need than Cat, on that cold December morning just six months ago. Her husband of 20 years had chosen Christmas Eve to announce that not only was he having an affair with someone young enough to be their daughter but he also wanted a quickie divorce so they could marry before their child was born. It had come as a terrible shock to Cat. She had never envisioned this affair.

One look at his face told her that he was 'in love' with this girl and there was so sense in trying to change his mind. She was determined to never let him know how devastated this news had left her. For years, she wanted a child only to be told that he was happy just as they were and he didn't want anyone or anything to spoil the life they had together. She had bought into his lie and now she was left alone to face the lonely consequences.

As she walked down the steep steps to the small strip of beach below the Annapolis home they had shared for those many years, she tried to put things into perspective and make plans for her now uncertain future. Tears began to well up in her eyes when she realized that her beloved home had now been sold and this would in all probability be the last time she walked down this path that she so loved. As she raised her eyes to look out across the Bay, her foot slid across the top of the sea sprayed stairs and she lost her balance. The last thing she remembered before she lost consciousness was the cry of a gull and the sight of the waves coming onto shore. Cat didn't know how long she lay there before help arrived. When she finally came to she was lying in a hospital bed with a strange man sitting in the chair by her bed. He was sandy haired with freckles that covered his entire face and warm hazel eyes. Not a handsome face but a nice face.

"I fell. Where am I and who are you?" she quietly asked rubbing her head.

"Yes. You took a very nasty fall but the doctors say you will be fine, just some bruising and stiffness. I found you there and called 911 for the ambulance. My name is Jeff Hunter. I just bought Cliff House just down from where you fell.

"Thank you, Mr. Hunter. I was alone in the house so it really is lucky that you happened to come by. I suppose it could have been much worse."

"It certainly could have been. Actually, I wasn't even on the beach this morning. If it hadn't been for that big dog of yours coming bounding out of nowhere and scaring me half to death then you would probably still be lying there or worse yet floating in the Bay."

Cat looked at him in confusion as he continued the story of her rescue.

"I tried shooing him away but he was so persistent. He kept running up to me and barking and then running toward the beach and looking back at me. I could almost swear he was waving me on toward you. Anyway, I finally got the idea that he wanted me to follow him. When I did, I found you there. He has lying beside you with that big head across you. He is amazing. That is some dog you have there," beamed Mr. Hunter.

"Mr. Hunter, what dog are you talking about? I don't own a dog."

"Perhaps it was a neighbor's dog that is fond of you?"

Cat was intrigued and asked, "What kind of dog was it Mr. Hunter and where is he now?"

"Blamed if I know, but he is one monster of a dog and he is at my house. I put him in the mudroom and gave him some food and water. I stopped at your house and there was no one there so I thought it was best and then I came straight over here to check on you. The doctor says you can be released as soon as someone can come pick you up."

"Oh, that might be a bit difficult," whispered Cat.

"Can I call your husband for you?"

"That might be even trickier. He's on vacation with his fiancée at the moment."

"Oh, I am sorry. The neighbors didn't mention that you were divorced."

"Well, it was just final today, so they wouldn't have known. As a matter of fact, today was meant to be my last visit to the house before the sale is finalized."

"Boy, he sure didn't waste any time, did he?" blurted out her rescuer. "Oh, I am sorry. It really isn't any of my business."

Cat started to giggle, "Well, at least you speak your mind and I admire honesty. It is so rare these days. I am really sorry that I am going to miss having you for a neighbor Mr. Hunter."

"Listen, I'm already here anyway and I am going your way. How about if I take you home and you can meet your real rescuer and maybe help me find out who he belongs to?"

"Thank you, Mr. Hunter. That is so very kind of you."

"OK then, let me get the nurse for you and we'll get you out of here in a jiffy," smiled Mr. Hunter.

"Oh, there is one thing, Mr. Hunter."

"Yes?"

"You're not an axe murderer or anything like that?"

"Certainly not. I'm a lawyer, and before you say another word. Yes, I have heard all the jokes."

As Mr. Hunter exited and the nurse entered with her follow up instructions, Cat slid out of the bed and reached for her clothes.

"Make sure that you follow the doctor's instructions carefully. If you have any bleeding from the nose, ears or mouth have someone bring you back immediately. You may have a headache for a day or two but Tylenol should take care of that. If it doesn't then you can come back to the emergency room. And stay indoors for the next couple of days and off those stairs to the beach," instructed the nurse.

"Yes, ma'am," replied Cat as she clicked her heels and mustered up her best salute for the nurse.

"Go on now. Out of here. We have really sick people waiting for this bed," teased the nurse.

As the nurse began to strip the bed and prepare for her next patient, Cat slipped out the door and walked down the hall to where Mr. Hunter waited at the nurses' station.

"All ready to go?" he asked as he offered her his arm.

"Yes, I believe so."

"Good, I have my car right out front so you don't have to walk too far."

"You are too kind. I can't thank you enough for taking time out of your day."

"It was you that I should thank," replied Mr. Hunter.

"Me?" questioned Cat.

"Yes, you saved me from a day of clearing brush. I hate to admit this but this is my first house and I didn't have a clue about how much work a garden was going to be, especially one that had been allowed to become so overgrown with brush."

"Ah yes, well you see, poor Mrs. Clark had been bedridden for months before she finally went into the nursing home and sadly passed away and there was no one to tend it. Both her sons live and work in New York City so they were hardly any use. If it is any consolation, she had the most beautiful garden when she was well and most of her plants were perennials so under that mess you should have some nice mature plants this spring."

"Umm, are you telling me that I maybe shouldn't be ripping everything out?"

"You haven't have you?"

"Well, see it is a blessing that I got distracted today, because I planned on doing that very thing. Perhaps, if you are feeling better later this week you could show me what to take out and what to leave?" pleaded Mr. Hunter.

He looked so pathetic and he had been so very kind to her that Cat quickly replied, "I will be delighted Mr. Hunter."

"Could you call me Jeff, please? Every time you say Mr. Hunter, I feel like looking around for my father."

Cat giggled and said, "And you may call me Catherine or Cat if you prefer."

"Cat it is then," beamed Jeff as he maneuvered his car through the narrow streets of Annapolis.

Chapter 3

For five months Cat lived in her rented townhome just across the narrow cobbled street from the market house which sat at the harbor's edge. Since coming here as a young bride, Cat had grown to love Annapolis. In the 20 years she had lived here nothing really seemed to change and constancy was one thing that Cat's personality thrived on. After the events of December, constancy was something Cat no longer had in her life and it had greatly affected her ability to finish her latest book. Writer's block was something that Cat had never totally believed in but after weeks of trying to come up with an ending for her third novel in the series she was a believer.

With the coming of spring, Cat spent most of her spare time at Jeff's house just two doors from the home that she had loved and lost. Jeff's garden needed a lot of work and Cat found that by keeping busy the uncertainty of the future didn't weigh so heavily on her mind. Then there was the matter of the dog that had saved her life. Her lease didn't allow dogs, especially one as large as this one, so he stayed with Jeff while they attempted to find his owner.

Jeff and Cat had contacted all of the local animal shelters and had placed advertisements in all the local papers but no one came forward to claim the big dog. So after another long night and way too many rounds at O'Brien's Pub, they decided to name the big dog The O'Brien.

It was on the same night, having returned from the pub, that Jeff checked his mail to find a letter from a solicitor in Dublin advising him that his elderly Aunt O'Bannon had left him her home in her will.

"Now, what am I going to do with another house and one in Ireland to boot? I've only been there once as a teenager with my mother when Uncle Patrick passed away," confided Jeff as he leaned forward to light Cat's after dinner cigarette.

"I'm so sorry to hear of your aunt's passing but what wouldn't I give for a letter like that? A free home and one in Ireland. What could be more perfect?" sighed Cat.

"Perfect? Do you really mean that you would just up and move to Ireland, just like that?"

"It would be a perfect time to do it. I could finally finish that book before my publisher disowns me and my lease is nearly up," mused Cat.

"And you would go there all alone not knowing anything about the place and not knowing anyone? And that's even if you would be allowed to immigrate there," pondered Jeff.

"Oh, there wouldn't be a problem with the immigration. My maiden name is Murphy and I have been using it since the divorce and since both my grandparents were born and raised in Sligo I could apply for citizenship under the Grandparent Clause. And as for me being alone," smiled Cat, as she reached down to pat the big dog lying at her feet, "The O'Brien could come with me. All he needs is his shots and a pet passport."

"Well, if you are seriously considering becoming my tenant, then you better get your paperwork in order because I have to let the solicitor in Dublin know what my plans are for the property. When would you want to go?" asked Jeff.

"Late May would be perfect, I think. It would give me enough time to go to the embassy, arrange for the shipment of my things and get O'Brien's paperwork in order."

"Now, that brings up an interesting subject," mused Jeff. "You see, as I recall the house is basically one large room downstairs and one bedroom and a bath upstairs in the loft with a staircase going up the middle."

Cat pondered for a moment trying to think of what she would do with the furniture she had collected over the years to fill the big house that she had shared with her former husband. As her eyes swept her friend's sparsely furnished family room a smile crept across her face.

"You know, Jeff, you really need to do something with this house. You've been here over five months and it still looks like it was furnished with your old dorm furniture. What in the world do the ladies think when you bring them back here after a date?"

"I don't actually bring any ladies back here to my house. Except you of course and you already knew what it looked like. But I suppose that you are right, I do need some proper furniture. Maybe you could sell me some that you won't need, if you are really intent on this venture."

"I really think that I am Jeff. I will miss you terribly but I think I need to get away from Annapolis. It's really difficult for me especially with my ex and his new family parading up and down Main Street every time I go out. I need to put some space between me and my past."

"Well then, if I can't change your mind, at least I know a good lawyer who will draw up your lease for practically nothing!" laughed Jeff.

Talking into the early hours of the morning, Jeff described the small harbor side village that Cat would be calling her new home.

"It reminds me a bit of Annapolis, except not so commercial," laughing Jeff continued. "Well, maybe I should have said not commercial at all. Since the EU put all the fishing restrictions in place there isn't a lot happening at the harbor. As I recall, most of the town depends on the big house for their livelihood. The last time I was there, the whole town consisted of a couple of shops that met the everyday needs of the town people, but for anything else you would have to go into Sligo."

"Big house?" asked Cat.

"Yeah, there is a manor house that sits just outside town. It's apparently been in the same family for generations and with owning over a thousand acres they employ half of the village. Those that don't work there depend a lot on trade from the manor to keep their businesses afloat."

"I think it's time for me to head home to bed," replied Cat as she yawned and climbed to her feet.

"Want a lift?"

"No thanks. It's only a few blocks and it's such a beautiful night so I'll walk," replied Cat as she gave Jeff a hug and closed the door behind her and headed toward home.

As she walked, she thought to herself, 'Ballysea sounds perfect. Might be just what I need.'

Chapter 4

Finishing her morning shopping Cat climbed the slight rise toward the cottage that she now called her home in Ballysea.

As she drew closer to the cottage she spotted a glisten of copper at her front door. Sitting patiently on her front doorstep was a young girl of about ten. Her beautiful shiny red hair shone like spun copper in the sunshine.

As she approached, the young girl jumped to her feet and bent to retrieve a woven basket that had been sitting beside her on the step.

"Good Morning Miss Murphy. My name is Caitlin O'Brien and I live over there in Rose Cottage," she said pointing to the neatly kept cottage at the far end of the lane. "My mother sent this along to welcome you to Ballysea and she says she hopes you will be very happy here and to call upon her if you need anything at all. You will be more than welcome in our home."

"My goodness, well thank you very much and thank your mother for me," smiled Cat as she took the basket that the child offered.

"May I introduce you to my friend and I do believe his name may be familiar to you," smiled Cat as she stepped aside and let O'Brien move to sit in front of the child.

"Caitlin O'Brien, this is my dear companion O'Brien and he would like to shake hands with you if you care to put out your right hand."

Caitlin cautiously put her small hand out and O'Brien quickly offered his paw while thumping his big tail in a noisy welcome.

"Oh miss. He's a big one isn't he? Is he always this nice and friendly?" squealed the young girl excitedly.

"Yes Caitlin, O'Brien truly loves children and would protect anyone he loved with all that is in him. He would never intentionally hurt anyone without very good cause," replied Cat.

With that, the sound of a bell ringing sent Caitlin running for home. "That would be my mammy calling us in for lunch," shouted the young girl as she flew down the path toward home.

"How many are there of you?" shouted Cat after the fleeing child.

"There are three others and then Da and Mam," shouted Caitlin over her shoulder as she bounded down the lane to home.

Peeking in the basket Cat mused," My goodness, three children, a husband to take care of, and a garden that looks glorious and she still has time to bake homemade bread and a cake to welcome a new neighbor. I must meet this superwoman."

And meet her she did. The very next day as Cat was starting to pour her second cup of coffee there was a gentle knock at the door. Opening the door wide, Cat looked up into the smiling freckled face of Maureen O'Brien.

"I haven't waken you or come at a bad time, have I?" she asked as she quickly introduced herself.

"Not at all. I have been up for hours and was just having a cup of coffee. Will you join me?" asked Cat.

"Oh yes, I'd love a cup of coffee and we can have one of these with it, if you like. I baked them this morning and I always seem to bake a few too many," replied Maureen as she pulled a bag of still warm scones from her apron.

The wonderful smell of the scones roused O'Brien from his bed by the open fire and he slowly rose and stretched out before lumbering over to meet their new neighbor.

"My goodness, he is as big as my Caitlin said. I thought for sure she must be exaggerating. Ah, you're a lovely big fellow aren't you and I understand that we're distant relatives aren't we my bonny fellow? We, O'Brien's must always stick together," she whispered as she gently stroked The O'Brien's big head.

"O'Brien never seems to meet a stranger, especially one bearing gifts of food," Cat replied as she poured the coffee and unconsciously reached for her pack of cigarettes.

"Oh, I am sorry Maureen. Does smoking bother you?" asked Cat.

"Actually, I love a nice cigarette with my morning coffee and was hoping that you might offer me one. I do enjoy the occasional cigarette but with having the children around the house in the morning I don't feel right about it."

And so it began the morning coffee, scones and cigarette exchange between two women who would grow to become lifelong friends and confidants.

Chapter 5

It was during one of these morning coffee breaks a week later that Maureen suggested a trip into Sligo to do some shopping in preparation for the long anticipated delivery of Cat's furniture and household goods.

"Let's see, we'll need to find you just that right color of yellow paint for your walls you've been talking about and some nice white for the trim. You'll want to get that done before your furniture arrives and I know just the right shop for paint and there's a linen shop close to it that carry the best lace curtains."

And so the plans were laid for the two friends and the O'Brien to begin a short journey that would culminate in revelations about the mysterious disappearance of one of the village's inhabitants.

The drive into town should have taken less than an hour but in the middle of the trip at the most desolate spot possible, Maureen's vintage Citroen 2CV decided to just quit. While Maureen poked around under the opened bonnet to try to get the little car to start again, Cat took the opportunity to expedite O'Brien from his rather cramped position in the small rear seat. Maureen had assured Cat that The O'Brien would fit in the back seat because after all farmers throughout Europe had been known to carry a sheep in them. Unfortunately for O'Brien, he was a bit bigger than the average sheep.

Once released from his confinement, O'Brien was off like a shot and exploring the terrain. Cat smiled as she watched her companion rolling in a field of wildflowers. "Well someone is really enjoying the beauty of Ireland today," she called to Maureen who was by now up to her elbows in engine grease.

"Jump in and try to start her now," called Maureen.

Just as Cat was sliding into the driver's seat, the screeching of breaks and a flurry of cursing met her ears.

"What the bloody Hell are you doing stopping your car in the middle of the road like this and on a curve to boot. You could have killed all of us! "

Before she had a chance to explain, an arm reached into the car and began to pull her from the driver's seat. Unfortunately for her assailant, he hadn't noticed that his outburst had drawn the attention of O'Brien, who now stood perched on the small rise above the road.

"Get your hands off me you idiot, our car has broken down," swore Cat angrily. The stranger began to move away, but it was too late. The sound of his mistress' distressed voice sent The O'Brien into action and 200 pounds of hound propelled himself through the air onto the intruder knocking him to the ground. Before Cat and Maureen could intervene, The O'Brien had the man pinned to the ground and was standing over him with teeth bared.

"Call off your beast, for God's sake!"

"Maureen, do you know this thug? asked Cat.

"I'm afraid so, Cat. May I introduce Lord Granville. His family own this land through which we've been taking a shortcut."

With one wave of Cat's hand, O'Brien grudgingly climbed off his captive and returned to his mistress' side but his steel gray eyes never left the stranger who was now getting up from the ground.

Brushing off his clothes and climbing back into his Land Rover, he simply turned to Maureen and said, "I'll send help once I reach the Manor."

Shaking her head Maureen giggled, "Well, looks like you certainly won't be receiving any welcome baskets from his Lordship

"What's his story anyway? Is he always so arrogant?"asked Cat as she stood with her hands on her hips staring after the receding vehicle.

"I'm afraid it's a very long story," sighed Maureen.

"Well, from the looks of things we may have a very long wait," smiled Cat as she patted the grass beside where she and O'Brien had sprawled.

Chapter 6

"There have been Granville's livings at the Manor longer than Ballysea has existed. The village actually grew up around the manor during the days when the peasants needed protection from invaders from the land and sea. When invaders attacked, the villagers sought refuge inside the walls of the manor. Later the village would serve to provide the cheap labor required for the smooth running of the manor house and the thousands of acres of farm land and forests. Today, many of the villagers still owe their livelihood to the Granville's, including my family," explained Maureen.

"I didn't know your husband worked there," responded Cat.

"Yes, Has done since he was young lad. He actually started working there with his father as an apprentice. Now, he takes care of the general repairs and upkeep of the house itself. With it being so old, it takes a lot of mending to keep the roof from leaking and the central heat working. So it's a full time job that keeps him busy all the time."

"Well, that still doesn't give him the right to manhandle me like that, the arrogant sod. He acted like a common thug."

"He's really the nicest member of the family. You should meet his brother, Edward. His American millionaire wife disappeared a few years back after rumors that she was going to divorce him and leave and take all her money with her. No one has seen or heard from her since."

"Didn't her family in the States come look for her?" asked Cat.

"She was an orphan. Both parents were killed in a private plane crash and she was barely 18 when Edward married her and brought her here to live. Poor little sad and timid thing," mused Maureen. "Everyone just assumed she had just escaped and was enjoying life away from Edward. You see, he wasn't a very good husband. The marriage was arranged by his father and wasn't a love match. Personally, I never bought the story. She would have never gone and left Marian."

"Wait, you've lost me. Who's Marian?"

"Sorry, Marian is Lillian's daughter. She was only four when Lillian disappeared. Lillian and her dog left the manor together the same night. So everyone just assumed that she took him with her. She was terribly fond of the dog and he was very protective of her. Matter of fact, I did hear a rumor that Edward had to have stitches on his hand and leg after a run-in with Boston a week before Lillian disappeared. Lillian used to spend a lot of time with the Widow O'Bannon. I think she was a grandmother figure to her. I would see her nearly every Saturday carrying baskets of food to her and then carrying coal in for her cooking and heat. She really doted on her and the widow loved her dearly. She was never the same after Lillian went missing. She behaved like she was haunted by something."

Just then a Land Rover appeared around the corner and two men climbed out. Maureen quickly climbed to her feet and warmly greeted the men.

"Hi Michael. Hi Sean. Thanks for coming so quickly. We were just heading into Sligo to pick up some paint and curtains when my car gave out.

Sorry, where are my manners? Have you met Catherine Murphy? She's just moved into the Widow O'Bannon's croft and this is her friend O'Brien," explained Maureen as Cat joined her at the front of the car with O'Brien.

"Nice to meet you, Miss and you big fellow," smiled Sean as Michael began poking around in the motor of the 2CV.

Taking a piece of cloth from his pocket, Michael began cleaning a spark plug that he had pulled from engine. "Here's your problem, let's get this cleaned up and see if we can get you moving and into town before those shops close. Maureen, jump behind the wheel and turn over the ignition and see if this works."

Maureen slide quickly behind the wheel and turned the key and after a few false starts the engine shook to life.

"Thanks so much for coming to our rescue and please thank Lord Granville for sparing you to help us."

"No problem at all ladies. Now, Maureen tell that husband of yours that you need new spark plugs and probably a good tune-up. Don't want to get stranded out here in bad weather. Nice to meet you Miss Murphy and welcome to our village. Hope you find what you are looking for here." And with a wave of their hands and a wink in Cat's direction they were off.

"Cheeky buggers," muttered a smiling Cat.

"Ah...they mean well. It's not often that we get fresh meat, if you'll excuse the expression, in our little village and eligible ladies are far and few between. Especially ones as attractive as you," smoothed Maureen.

"Well, if you put it that way," laughed Cat again. "So, tell me more about this Lord Granville."

"Oh, I thought you weren't interested in our local thug," smiled Maureen as she raised an eyebrow in Cat's direction.

"Well, he is the best looking thug I have had the pleasure of being man handled by in years," giggled Cat.

Chapter 7

Wandering to the front door of her cottage, Cat threw open the door and raising her cup of coffee to her mouth looked out across the green fields that sloped to the quiet gray sea below. With the mist still clinging to the grass everything took on a softer less real appearance. She could just picture what it must have been like in the days that this was still a bustling fishing harbor with a daily market. She wondered if the village would ever have a market again. 'Even a weekly one where the locals could sell their specialty food and wares would be a bonus to village life,' she thought.

Looking down at the neglected flower bed she stroked O'Briens head and mused, "Looks like a good day to make a start on the garden, my friend, but breakfast first, huh? Got to keep our energy up, don't we?"

The smell of the thick slabs of Irish bacon sizzling away in the pan kept The O'Brien sitting eagerly by the ancient stove as Cat puttered around the kitchen.

Breakfast done, Cat slipped into her tattered old baggy jeans and pulled on her wellies and was ready for a go at the long neglected garden. Kneeling down, Cat began to attack the weeds closest to the front door and as if trying to help her, O'Brien moved around to the side of the house and began to sniff around and then dig excitedly.

"Boy, you are really getting into this gardening thing, aren't you?" Cat laughed as she watched the dirt being thrown from the hole that O'Brien was attacking with a vengeance. Suddenly, he stopped and began to whimper in a way that Cat had never heard. Jumping up and hurrying to the side of the cottage Cat reached for O'Brien's paw and asked, "What is it big fellow? Have you hurt yourself?"

As Cat bent down to examine his paws, her eyes caught the glimmer of something laying half buried in the dirt. It looked like a piece of silver jewelry. Thinking she had found a lost treasure or ancient artifact, she carefully reached into the dirt and hooking a finger through the object, began to

slowly pull it from the earth. Within seconds she
stopped cold. At the end of the object was what
appeared to be the partial skeleton of a small
animal.

"Oh my, O'Brien. We seemed to have disturbed
someone's pet cemetery."

Cat began to quickly excavate a little more of the
grave so she could safely return the remains to
where they had been buried those many years
when she noticed the name on the silver tag. It
was Boston. A chill ran through her body as she
recalled how Maureen had told her about the
disappearance of Lillian Granville and her little
dog. What was the poor creature doing buried
here and what caused its death and if his mistress
never went anywhere without him then where was
she?

"You've done wonders with this place," called a
familiar voice.

Rising from her kneeling position and brushing the
dirt from her hands on her jeans, Cat smiled and
turned to see which of the friendly villagers had

stopped to have a chat. Her smile soon disappeared when she came face to face with Lord Granville.

"Lord Granville," muttered Cat as she thought back on their last less than friendly encounter and felt the hairs on the back of her neck start to rise.

Cat was just about to tell him exactly how she felt about his attitude of entitlement and his arrogate manner when a young girl, ran up to join them and grabbed his hand.

"Uncle Ryan, may I pet the big doggy, oh please?

"You'll have to ask the nice lady. He's her dog," replied her uncle as he smiled down at the child and tousled her dark curly hair.

"Please miss, may I? He doesn't bite does he?"

"Of course you may pet him. O'Brien loves children and he might be very big but he is also very gentle as well as protective of those he loves," replied Cat gently as she gave Lord Granville a meaningful look.

Stretching his hand out to Cat, he said softly, "I do hope you won't hold my bad behavior the other day against me. I'm not usually so bad tempered. I am truly sorry."

"Apology accepted," replied Cat taking his hand and shaking it firmly. "And who is this charming little one?" as she peeked over to see O'Brien lavishing all his attention on the young girl.

"She's my niece Marian. My brother's child," replied Lord Granville.

Smiling over at the child, Cat said, "She's lovely and she seems to have a very gentle way with animals."

"Yes, she is very much like her mother. She was a gentle soul. Beautiful both inside and out and a real animal lover," spoke Lord Granville wistfully.

"Marian, we had better get on. You'll be late for your friend's birthday party," called her uncle quickly changing the subject. Cat couldn't help but notice that the mention of Lillian Granville had triggered an emotion response from the younger of the Granville brothers.

"Well, it was nice chatting with you Lord Granville," said Cat.

"Please, it's Ryan. I hope that you will find everything you are looking for here and if there is anything I can help you with, you just need to ask."

"Ryan it is then," smiled Cat.

Cat watched as they made their way down the lane to the village and raised her hand and waved as he turned to look back at her before disappearing around a corner.

Going back to O'Brien's discovery, Cat slowly covered the remains with dirt and thought to herself that she had already found one thing that she really wasn't looking for. Now the question was, what was she going to do about it and who could she trust with the news of their gruesome discovery.

Cat passed a restless night dreaming about the remains and wrestling with the implications of the find and who she could safely tell.

Shuffling into the kitchen at daybreak she fixed a cup of strong coffee, dropped into the closest chair and lighting a cigarette reached for the telephone.

"Jeff, it's Cat. Can you get some time away from your practice? I really need someone over here that I can trust completely," asked Cat quietly.

"Of course Cat but what is it? Are you OK?" stammered Jeff.

"Yes, Jeff. I'm fine. I just need someone that I can trust. Someone to listen and help me sort out a mystery that appears to have landed on my proverbial doorstep. When can you come?"

Jeff quickly logged onto his laptop and began to search for available flights.

"OK. I managed to get the last seat on British Airways leaving tonight. I'll be in London Heathrow before 10:00 am and then I'll catch the first available flight into Shannon. I'll get a rental car and be with you just as quickly as possible. You'll be safe until I get there won't you Cat? I'm really worried now."

"I'll be fine Jeff, thanks for coming so quickly and please don't worry. I'm in no danger. I just need someone with your analytical mind."

Chapter 8

On the other side of Ballysea, there was another that was passing a restless night. Ryan Granville was having a difficult time keeping the image of the lovely blond newcomer from his dreams since their conversation the day before. Ryan hadn't had much time to think about the fairer sex since the disappearance of his sister-in-law and the abandonment of his brother's parental duties.

Rising early, Lord Granville stepped into his jeans and pulling the heavy Aran knit sweater over his head rushed downstairs for his morning cup of tea.

Mrs. O'Malley, who had been the manor housekeeper since Ryan was a young lad, was already up and moving about the kitchen. "The kettle's boiled, Master Ryan. Fix yourself a cuppa. I'm off to check on the wee one," she hollered as she climbed up the stone back staircase that lead from the kitchen to the family rooms above. In the days when the manor had been fully staffed these were the steps used by the butler and the footman to carry food from the massive kitchen to the elegant dining room above stairs.

Mrs. O'Malley had walked up to the gates of the manor soon after Ryan and Edward's mother's death and asked for work. Her fisherman husband had been lost at sea leaving her a young widowed mother with five small children to feed and clothe. The old Lord Granville had seen something in this woman's manner that told him this woman was someone the manor desperately needed.

Ryan smiled as he remembered how from the very first day, the gloom that had filled the manor during his mother's long illness and death had miraculously lifted. Perhaps it was the laughter of her own children that filled the kitchen as she worked or perhaps it was simply the smell of the home baked bread that lifted the spirits of the entire household. But whatever it was, it seemed like a miracle to the youngest Granville. The elder Lord Granville was once again completely free to manage his vast estate and make the improvements that his late wife's large insurance policy now afforded.

Pouring himself a cup of tea and walking across the freshly scrubbed slate floors, Ryan opened the kitchen door to gaze across the courtyard to the hills and town beyond. He loved the morning sounds and smells. The birds singing their own distinct morning songs mingling with the soft smell of the peat fires from the crofts of the manor workers brought a smile to his face.

With the Manor Open Days rapidly approaching next weekend, Ryan knew that he should be taking care of organizing the events and the catering setup but his mind kept going back to his dreams about Cat.

Dumping the last of his tea into the climbing rose bush by the kitchen door he called, "Mrs. O'Malley, I'm running into town. Can I bring you anything?"

"No lad. Just don't you be too long. We have a lot to get through today," called Mrs. O'Malley as she walked back into the warm kitchen.

Coming through town, he passed Maureen struggling up the hill with her shopping.

"Morning Maureen! Can I give you a lift home?" called Ryan as he pulled the Range Rover up alongside her.

"Hey Ryan! Yes please, that would be lovely. I wasn't sure these eggs were going to make it home without ending up scrambled," laughed Maureen as she climbed into the front seat beside Ryan.

Maureen was surprised to see Ryan in town today and asked, "What brings you into town today? I thought you'd be home setting up for the Open Day this weekend."

"I needed to check on a few things and I thought I might just as well stop in at Cat's and extend her an invitation," replied Ryan as he pulled up in front of Maureen's cottage.

"Oh, looks like Cat has company." said Maureen as she climbed out of the Land Rover and nodded towards the Croft.

Ryan turned his head just in time to witness Cat exchanging enthusiastic hugs on her front door step with a strange man carrying a suitcase.

"Well, I won't disturb them. Could you mention to her about the Open Day plans? Maybe if she isn't too busy, then she and The O'Brien can come along. Marian would love a chance to spend some time with that dog again."

Maureen knew Ryan well enough to know it was him that wanted to spend time with a certain party and it surely wasn't The O'Brien.

"I'll be glad to, Ryan. I'll be seeing you on the weekend," she replied.

Smiling to herself Maureen thought, 'And I know a jealous man when I see one.'

Chapter 9

"So what's happened that you didn't want to discuss with that new best friend of yours I keep hearing about?" asked Jeff faking hurt feelings.

"Don't be silly. Maureen is my best friend but you saved my life and that gives you special status well beyond best friend," smiled Cat as she gave Jeff one last hug.

"Have you eaten? I was just going to fix some breakfast. How was the flight?" asked Cat as she headed for the stove.

"Flight was fine. But if you call a half frozen, stale tasting muffin and a cup of mud which the airline passes off as coffee breakfast, then yes. But I would love some real coffee and maybe some toast," replied Jeff as he dropped into a chair and watched Cat move around the small kitchen. He couldn't help but notice how much she had changed in such a short time. 'This place must really agree with her. She looks ten years younger,' he thought.

At that precise moment Cat turned to catch Jeff staring at her, "You're staring at me Mr. Hunter. Have I grown another eye in the middle of my forehead or something?" giggled Cat as she passed Jeff his coffee.

"Actually, I was thinking that you have done wonders with this place. It looks great. And I couldn't help but notice that you look great too. This place must really agree with you," replied Jeff.

"Thank you. I have been busy and I'm very happy with the way everything has turned out. I do like it here. I'm just worried about my little find," replied Cat as her voice took on an ominous tone.

"What find, Cat? You act like you found a dead body or something," laughed Jeff as he lifted his coffee to his lips.

"Well, not exactly a body. It was a skeleton," replied Cat.

Jeff began choking on his coffee, "A skeleton? Here in the house? For god sake, Cat. Did you call the Garda?" stammered Jeff as he wiped the now dripping coffee from his chin and stared around the croft.

"Not inside. Actually, O'Brien found it in the side garden and it wasn't human," replied Cat.

"Not human? Then what was it?" asked Jeff.

"A dog," Cat replied solemnly.

Jeff was on his feet by now, "A dog? You had me drop everything and fly over here because O'Brien dug up someone's dead pet dog?" demanded Jeff.

"That's the problem, Jeff. It just wasn't anyone's pet dog. Oh, perhaps I should start at the beginning," sighed Cat.

Cat spent the better part of the next hour telling Jeff about the unexplained disappearance of Marian's mother and the strange behavior of her father.

"I understand now why you didn't want to talk about this with the locals. As I told you before, the Granville's do employ half the village and the rest of them depend on their goodwill to keep their businesses afloat," mused Jeff.

"Well, according to Maureen the dog was always with its mistress and I just cannot believe that she went off and abandoned her child. I think she was murdered, Jeff," whispered Cat.

Chapter 10

Long into the early morning hours of the next day, Jeff and Cat sat curled up on the sofa in front of the open fire trying to unravel the mystery of the young Lady Granville's sudden disappearance. The glow from the dying embers mesmerized the jet lagged Jeff until he finally said, "I'm sorry Cat but I need sleep. Tomorrow is another day and we can start trying to find the answers to what happened to Marian's mother and her pet dog."

"You take my bed, Jeff. I'm more than happy to sleep here in front of the fire with O'Brien." At the mention of his name, O'Brien crossed the room and collapsed at his mistress' feet and let out a huge sigh.

"I do believe we are keeping someone from his beauty sleep," laughed Jeff as he climbed the stairs to Cat's loft bedroom. Throwing his clothes onto the arm chair, Jeff climbed into the feather bed and pulled the down comforter over him and was asleep in what seemed like seconds.

Downstairs, sleep still eluded Cat. Pouring a glass of scotch, she opened the window, lit a cigarette and stared out at the sea below. Staring out into the dark night, she wondered if she would ever be able to find the answer to what had happened and how the little dog had come to be buried beside the croft. Perhaps the answer lay in the friendship that had developed between the old widow and the young American heiress. At least that was a starting point. Tomorrow when Maureen stopped in for her morning coffee she would try to find out some more about the odd relationship.

Dropping the remains of her cigarette into the fireplace grate, Cat curled up on the sofa and pulling the throw over her finally fell into a fitful asleep. Visions of a woman clutching a bundle in her arms as she ran along the shoreline haunted her dreams until everything faded to black as Cat finally fell into a deep sleep.

The smell of freshly brewed coffee stirred Cat from her sleep as she opened her eyes to find Jeff and O'Brien starring at her in anticipation.

Stretching and yawning, Cat mumbled, "I suppose this means that my favorite two guys are hungry and it's time for me to get up and cook some breakfast. Has O'Brien been out for his morning run?"

"Yes. All taken care of. We had a nice walk on the beach, didn't we old boy? The town hasn't changed much since I was last here except maybe the harbor. Not many fishing boats around anymore," replied Jeff patting The O'Brien.

At the mention of breakfast, The O'Brien began jumping around excitedly and ran to take his place by the old oak farmhouse table that took up half the room in the kitchen.

"I thought I should get up and make myself presentable for when your neighbor comes over for her morning coffee," replied Jeff as he handed Cat a cup of coffee. As I recall, "two sugars and milk, right?"

"Perfect. Thanks Jeff. I really need a strong cup of coffee this morning. Boy, what dreams I had last night," replied Cat. Before she could continue with her story, O'Brien's tail started thumping loudly followed by a light knock at the door.

"Can you get that, Jeff? " yelled Cat as she ran up the stairs to get a quick shower and change out of the clothes that she had slept in.

Opening the door, Jeff smiled at Maureen and said, "Come on in Maureen. We've been expecting you. Cat is in the shower but she'll be right down. Can I get you a coffee? Oh, by the way, I'm Jeff Hunter, Cat's old neighbor in the States and her landlord here."

Maureen smiled back at Jeff and replied, "I know exactly who you are. We met when you were over for your uncle's funeral."

"Are you sure? I am sure that I wouldn't forget someone as lovely as you," replied Jeff.

Before she could answer, Cat came bounding down the stairs, "Take it easy with that sweet talk Jeff. Maureen's a happily married lady."

"Ahhh, it's just the Irish coming out in him," replied Maureen as she smiled at her friend and placed a basket on the table.

"I saw your lights on late last night so I thought I would spare you having to cook this morning."

Inside the basket were bacon butties, scones, clotted cream and Maureen's wild strawberry jam. There was even an extra bacon butty for The O'Brien who sat eagerly thumping his big tail on the slate floor.

Cat spread the food Maureen had so thoughtfully brought onto the table and as they all settled down to enjoy their breakfast, Jeff asked Maureen to tell him about the final years of his aunt's life.

Chapter 11

Grabbing a napkin to wipe the butter dripping down her chin from the bacon butty, Maureen looked at Jeff and said sadly, "You know your aunt was never the same after your Uncle Patrick passed. They were married for such a very long time and a more devoted couple you'll never find. Everyone in town tried to pull her out of her depression but I think it was Lillian and her little dog that seemed to help the most."

Between bites she explained to Jeff, "Lillian was the wife of the old Lord Granville's oldest son Edward. Shy little thing she was and very attached to your aunt. Maybe it was because she was so far from her home in America or that her mother and father had died in that crash that drew her to your aunt. As you well remember, your aunt was a very mothering type and was very kind to everyone. Anyway, soon after your Uncle Patrick passed, we noticed that Lillian's daily walk with her little dog Boston on the beach now ended with a stop at the Croft. At first, when your aunt was able we would see the two of them walking into town arm and arm with Boston at their side.

Then later when her health declined, Lillian and Boston would come daily to bring her coal for her fire and baskets of food. Sometimes she'd even bring her daughter Marian. Lillian nursed your aunt until the day she just up and disappeared."

"Disappeared? You mean she just left without a word? What about her daughter and the dog? asked Jeff.

"Well, that is the strange part. She left them both. Marian still lives at the manor and is cared for mostly by her uncle and the housekeeper," replied Maureen as she reached for a scone.

"What about the dog?" Jeff asked.

"Boston disappeared from the manor on the same night as Lillian but days later he was seen wandering up and down the seafront until the butcher Mr. Burke was able to tempt him with some beef cubes. Your aunt insisted that the dog stay with her even though she wasn't really able to care for him. My Caitlin would go walk him a couple times a day and Mr. Burke saw that there were always plenty of scraps for him to eat. Then one day, he got loose from the house and the next thing we knew, his little body was found in the early hours of the morning laying there at your aunt's front door. My husband said that it looked like someone had rung his poor little neck."

"Dear lord, that is horrible," gasped Cat. "Who would do such a thing?"

Taking a cigarette from Cat's pack, Maureen lit it and exhaling the smoke replied, "Lillian's husband, that bastard Edward, of course. Everyone knew it but no one could prove it. We figured that Boston had gone back to the manor when he got lose and that Edward had killed him."

Maureen reached out and took Jeff's hand, "The day we buried him outside in her garden, is the very day that your dear aunt died. I think losing her husband, the disappearance of the girl she had grown to love like a daughter and the terrible manner in which poor Boston died was just too much for her aging heart."

"Well, that solves the mystery of Cat's find," replied Jeff thoughtfully.

81

"Find? What find, Cat?" asked Maureen.

"Well, the other day The O'Brien and I started to clear out the gardens around the house and I'm afraid that The O'Brien must have sensed something was there that wasn't just weeds and dug up the remains of Boston," replied Cat.

"Oh. I am sorry Cat. I should have mentioned it. We did have a small marker on the spot but that soon disappeared too. It was just like someone wanted to wipe out any reminders of Lillian or her little Boston," replied Maureen.

"So, what about Lillian?" Jeff asked.

"No word from her since she disappeared. Rumor has it that she just up and vanished because she couldn't stand living with Edward anymore. Some say there was something going on between Lillian and Edward's younger brother, Ryan. Others say she just up and moved back to America. There are even some that believe she never really left Ballysea," whispered Maureen.

"What do you think Maureen? Cat asked.

Maureen replied in a hushed tone, "I don't know for sure. But I can tell you one thing and that is, no good mother would leave their only young child with someone like Edward. And Lillian was a very good mother."

Fearing that she may have said too much Maureen suddenly reached for her now empty basket and said, "Look at the time. I must be getting home. Oh and before I forget, Ryan stopped by yesterday as Jeff was just arriving and asked me to invite you both and The O'Brien, of course, to the Open Day events at the Manor this weekend."

Escorting her friend to the door, Cat warmly hugged Maureen, "Thanks for the breakfast. It was lovely. See you tomorrow."

Closing the door behind her, and returning to sit with Jeff, Cat says, "Well, that's part of the mystery solved but now I'm even more convinced that Lillian never left Ballysea. What do you think big fellow? " asked Cat as she reached down and stroked The O'Brien's massive head.

83

"I don't know about him but I am inclined to agree with you," replied Jeff as he walked to the window and quietly watched Maureen cross the road to her cottage.

Chapter 12

The next two days passed quickly for Cat and Jeff as they caught up on all the gossip from back home in Annapolis and made plans to solve the mystery of the disappearance of Lillian Granville. Their morning ritual of coffee with Maureen continued but after her reaction when questioned about Lillian they decided not to broach the subject with her again. After all, her husband worked for the Granville's and her family's livelihood depended on their good will.

Saturday morning dawned bright and sunny just in time for the Manor Open Day. Cat had only seen the manor from a distance and as Jeff drove up the long drive she was amazed at the very size of it. Made of local stone it was a three story rectangular building almost completely covered in Virginia Creeper with a massive red door. The 100 acre parkland surrounding the manor was absolutely breathtaking. As they wound their way closer to the house they could see large tents spread across the side lawn as well as a variety of amusement rides for the village children. It looked like the Granville's had gone all out for this special event.

"I'll let you out here and go park the car then O'Brien and I will be right with you, "said Jeff as he brought the car to a stop by the side door of the manor.

As Cat waited by the side door of the manor, she heard shouting coming from within.

"You're drunk! I don't know why you bother to show up today of all days and drunk at that," Cat immediately recognized the voice of Ryan Granville.

"Because it's my manor and my land and I'll bloody well do as I please and if you don't like it little brother then you know what you can do" yelled the other person. It was now only too obvious to Cat that this must be the elder brother, Edward, she had heard so much about.

Then another calmer voice was heard, "The last time I checked Edward, I was a cripple but I'm not dead yet so this is still my manor and my land and if you don't like it then you know what you can do."

With that, the door flew open and Edward came stumbling out and weaving across the drive in her direction with a drunken leer on his face.

"What have we here? This isn't a face from the village that I recognize," sputtered Edward as put his hands on her shoulders to balance himself.

"If I were you, I would remove your hands," said Cat as she saw The O'Brien lower his head as he slowly moved in her direction.

Edward laughed as he replied, "Really, are you going to make me little lady?"

"No, but I'm afraid that my companion might." Cat could see the giant dog approaching silently across the drive with Jeff right behind him.

"Well, bring him on," shouted Edward as his fingers dug into her shoulders.

With just the movement of Cat's hand, The O'Brien was on Edward. As his massive paws connected with Edward's shoulders the sheer size of him forced the drunken man off of his feet and onto his back in seconds.

"Get him off me or I'll wring his bloody neck," he yelled.

Jeff and Cat exchanged a meaningful look while Ryan dragged Edward to his feet as the villagers crowded around watching the spectacle.

"Edward, you will apologize to the lady immediately," echoed a stern voice from the doorway.

Cat turned to see an elderly man in a wheelchair at the door to the manor. With a switch of a button, the motorized wheelchair moved to stop in front of where Cat stood.

Edward looked over at the elderly man and hanging his head muttered, "Sorry" before staggering back inside the manor.

Holding out a shaking hand to Cat, "I apologize for my son. I will see that he doesn't bother you again. I do hope this hasn't ruined your visit here today. My son Ryan will be glad to show you around the manor. Please don't hesitate to let him know if there is anything you need."

"Thank you very much sir. I'm sure that I'll enjoy my day here," replied Cat as the elder Granville maneuvered the wheelchair slowly back into the manor.

Cat leaned down and stroked O'Brien's head as Ryan spoke quietly to the gathered crowd, "Nothing more to see here everyone. Food and drinks are being served in the tents and rides for all the children, so please go and enjoy yourselves."

Crossing to her side, Ryan said, "Well, you've met the whole dysfunctional Granville family now. I do hope you and your friend will stay. Marian has been looking forward to visiting with The O'Brien again."

"Of course we will stay Ryan. May I introduce you to Jeff Hunter, my best friend from home?"

Jeff put his hand out and shaking Ryan's hand spoke softly, "Nice to meet you Ryan. Please don't worry about your brother's behavior. Trust me, in my line of work I have seen far worse."

Smiling at last, Ryan took his hand and asked, "Really? And what line of work might that be?"

Cat couldn't help smiling as she replied for her friend, "He's a criminal lawyer."

Ryan smiled too and the three of them and The O'Brien went off in search of Marian.

The rest of the day went smoothly and despite himself Ryan found himself truly enjoying Jeff's company. The two men talked easily together and before the end of the day they had already made plans to get together at the local pub the next evening. Cat strolled slowly behind observing the two men that were polar opposites in so many ways. Jeff looked the image of his Irish ancestry with his red hair and freckles while Ryan's black hair and blue eyes belied his French heritage. Jeff was calm and analytic while Ryan had shown himself to be erratic and impulsive.

Marian was delighted to see The O'Brien again and eagerly showed him off to all her young friends. Cat smiled as she watched the big dog rolling over onto his back so he could get the belly rubs that he loved from all the village children.

The rest of the day could have been perfectly idyllic hadn't the words, 'I'll wring his neck' not been constantly ringing in her ears as she kept a mindful eye on The O'Brien.

Chapter 13

The sound of O'Brien softly snoring was the first thing that Cat heard when she woke the next morning. Reaching down from her temporary bed on the couch, she gently patted his big head. "How's my big fellow this morning, eh? Ready for a quick walk on the beach before Jeff wakes up?"

O'Brien lumbered to his feet and padded over to the door as Cat stepped into her jeans and wellies and pulled a sweater over her head.

"Ready big guy?" laughed Cat as O'Brien danced around in front of the door. As soon as the door was open, he was out like a shot stopping only at the road to wait for Cat. Once on the beach he was free to run and play. Cat loved the beach nearly as much as The O'Brien. As the waves gently lapped against the shore, Cat found her thoughts going back to the scene at the Manor yesterday and the elder Lord Granville. The drunken bully Edward seemed genuinely frightened of his wheelchair bound father. Ryan had described the family as dysfunctional, yet while his father seemed nice enough the obvious fear on Edward's face when confronted by him raised a red flag to Cat.

Dropping down on one of the large boulders that ran from the cliff face toward the sea, Cat waited patiently for The O'Brien to return from his wanderings.

As she closed her eyes and breathed in the fresh sea air Cat mused, 'Maybe tonight at the pub, Jeff can find out more about Edward and his father.' Cat's brief moment of calm was abruptly interrupted by the frenzied barking of O'Brien.

Immediately, Cat was up and running in the direction of The O'Brien's barks. As she ran down the beach, Edwards Granville's words, 'I'll ring his bloody neck' kept ringing in her ears. Rounding a bend, she saw The O'Brien with his head stuck inside some thickets close to the beach. "O'Brien! What have you gotten yourself into now?" hollered Cat breathing a sigh of relief as she quickly approached.

Reaching down to pull O'Brien's head back she was surprised to see that the thickets appeared to cover the entrance to a sea cave. Cat was certain there must to be something in there or The O'Brien wouldn't have alerted her by barking like that. Grabbing O'Brien by his collar, Cat pulled him away from the thicket, "Come on big guy. Let's get home and rouse Jeff from his bed and get a flashlight and something to clear this brush away so we can see what you have discovered."

Dragging a reluctant O'Brien from the beach by his collar, Cat heard the familiar voice of her friend Maureen calling to her from her open front door. "Oh my, has someone been a bad boy?" laughed Maureen at the sight of Cat struggling to drag the massive O'Brien back home.

"Morning! Not really, but he seems to have discovered some sort of cave down at the beach that has attracted his attention. Just look at the state of him!" laughed Cat as she reached down trying to pull the pieces of brush from his wiry fur.

"A sea cave? I didn't know there were any sea caves that close to the village. I've seen some further up the coast that according to legend were used by pirates to store their looted bounty but none close to Ballysea," replied Maureen.

"I was just going up to get Jeff and a flashlight and have a look. Want to join us?"

"I would but I have my scones in the oven. How about I meet you in about an hour at your place and you can tell me what you find over coffee and scones?"

"Sounds good. I'll see you then," yelled Cat over her shoulder as she continued dragging O'Brien up the walk to her cottage.

Jeff was already awake and having his coffee as he watched Cat dragging O'Brien up the walk. Holding the door open for her he asked, "Now what has our friend here gotten himself into so early in the morning? Annoying the sea gulls again?"

"Not quite. Seems he has discovered a sea cave and I am sure there must be something in there or he wouldn't have been so intent on getting into it. Maureen said that pirates were known to hide their treasures in caves like this. It's covered with some heavy brush so we'll need to clear that and take a flashlight and have a look," replied Cat.

"Well, there's no time like the present!"

Slipping out of her wellies, Cat yawned and headed for the kitchen, "Coffee first then we can search for pirate booty."

Chapter 14

Gardening shears and flashlight in hand with The O'Brien leading the way, Cat and Jeff headed down the path to the beach. Not even taking time to chase the gulls, O'Brien was first to reach the cave entrance.

"No wonder no one knew about this cave. Look at this growth. And it looks like at high tide this cave could well be partially underwater. Good thing we came when we did," remarked Jeff as he started to cut the undergrowth away.

Once the opening was clear enough, O'Brien pushed his way into the small cave.

Shining the flashlight in through the small opening Cat urged, "Get some more of this cut away so we can get in there. Looks like O'Brien has found something."

O'Brien had indeed found something and was busy using his big paws to uncover it.

Once Jeff had cleared an opening large enough for Cat's slender frame, she entered the cave.

With flashlight in hand Cat knelt beside The O'Brien. Looking down she knew right away what O'Brien had found.

"What's he found? Pirate Booty?" yelled Jeff half laughing.

Cat replied in a hushed voice, "No. I think you need to run up to Maureen's and have her phone the Garda."

"Garda?"

"Yes. Looks like O'Brien has uncovered some bones and if I'm not sadly mistaken, they appear to be human," replied Cat solemnly.

Jeff dropped the shears and ran as fast as he could to Maureen's as Cat dragged O'Brien away from the partially exposed skeleton.

Speaking softly to O'Brien, Cat whispered, "Well done, big fellow. I think that you may have solved the mystery of the missing Lady Granville. Now it's up to the Garda and their pathologist to determine what happened to her and how she ended up here."

When Maureen and Jeff returned, Cat and O'Brien were sitting in the sand outside of the cave watching as the water began to rise and trickle slowly into the cave.

"How long do you think it will be before they get here?" asked Cat.

Looking at her watch, Maureen replied, "They are coming from Sligo so I would guess at least a half hour or maybe a little less."

"I wouldn't worry about it Cat, nothing can be done for the poor soul now," injected Jeff.

"I know. I was just thinking about whether they would get here before the tide comes in and the cave is underwater again," replied Cat.

Twenty minutes passed in what seemed like an eternity to Cat when the sound of sirens met her ears. Climbing up to the road from the beach, Jeff flagged down the two patrol cars and directed them to where Cat and Maureen sat on the beach.

The older of the officers, a heavy-set man of about 45 with a weathered face and graying hair asked, "Which of you ladies discovered the remains."

Cat responded as she pointed to The O'Brien, "Actually, it was neither of us but The O'Brien here. He actually found the cave during our morning walk on the beach and alerted us that there was something he needed us to see inside. So my friend Jeff and I cleared the brush away and I went in after O'Brien to find him uncovering the remains."

The younger of the officers reached over and stroked O'Brien's head and remarked, "He's smart as well as handsome then."

Cat responded as she had so many times before, "The O'Brien has an uncanny way of helping people in need and now I guess that extends to those dead as well as those living."

The younger and thinner of the two officers squeezed his way through the small opening and called out to his partner, "Human remains sir and they appear to be female. We'll need to get a forensic team in here to excavate the remains."

"With the tide coming in, it looks like it is going to have to wait until the morning because this cave is going to be under water soon," called the older officer.

"We'll need to cordon off the area for today and have a guard stand by to keep any curious onlookers away until the team can get here tomorrow morning when it's low tide," continued the officer as he began to set up the perimeter.

"We'll need to question each of you later today, if that is convenient," continued the officer.

"I live just up the hill and we'll all be there for the next hour if that works for you," responded Cat as she pointed her cottage out to the officer.

"That would be fine. We'll be right up as soon as we cordon off the area and call for a guard"

"Coffee, Maureen?" asked Cat.

"Yes, please and I could murder for a cigarette this morning," relied Maureen as she opened her front door and collected the plate of scones she baked that morning.

Trying to make light of their discovery, Jeff winked at Maureen and said, "Very poor choice of words after the events of this morning."

Chapter 15

"So, do you really think that could be Lillian Granville's remains," asked Maureen as she took a deep drag off her second cigarette.

"The officer said they appear to be female but I guess we'll just have to wait and see if there is anything to identify the remains or even how the poor soul died," replied Jeff as he watched the pensive face of Cat.

Cat watched as her friend nervously twisted her long red hair with her other free hand and wondered what was going through her mind.

Finally, Maureen asked, "Do you think we should let anyone up at the manor know?"

The lawyer in Jeff quickly replied, "Not until the officials make a positive identification. There is nothing to say for sure that those are her remains and whoever it is we don't know if it was an accidental death or murder. What I'm saying is, we really shouldn't say anything that could interfere with the police investigation or worry loved ones unnecessarily."

"I agree. It will be all over the village by this evening anyway once the beach is cordoned off but it's really a matter for the Garda now. The least said the best," replied Cat.

Their conversation was abruptly interrupted by a firm knock on the door announcing the arrival of the two officers.

"Coffee?" asked Cat.

"Yes ma'am. That would be lovely," replied the younger and more congenial of the two officers.

As they settled around the old oak table, the older more senior officer addressed them, "We would appreciate it if you didn't discuss the events of this morning with anyone until after our team has a chance to determine the identity and cause of death of the victim. I know this village very well and I can guarantee you that the minute that our cars leave the front of your house half the town's people will be here asking you questions. We are also more than familiar with village gossip surrounding the case of Lillian Granville's disappearance but again we ask that you not discuss your find with anyone, especially anyone connected to the manor."

With that last remark the officer looked directly at Maureen. "As I recall, Mrs. O'Brien, your husband works up at the manor so I am asking you not to discuss anything about this morning with him."

Maureen simply bowed her head and nodded her agreement.

After drinking their coffee and taking statements from all three, the officers left and returned to the beach.

"Wow. How am I not going to say anything to my own husband?" asked Maureen.

"I really wouldn't worry about you having to keep the secret. I noticed old Mary McIntyre watching and listening to everything that was going on from her front step. If I'm not mistaken everyone from here to Sligo probably has heard the news by now," giggled Cat.

Jeff laughed, "Of the best means of communication, telephone, telegraph and tell a woman. The last is the fastest or so Uncle Patrick always claimed. I think he must have been referring to old Mary."

With that last remark, Maureen was up and out the door to get home and finish her housework before the rest of the family returned home for their evening meal.

As she watched her friend make her way across the lane to her cottage, Cat turned to Jeff and asked, "What do you make of Maureen's behavior?"

"Well, she did seem very nervous," replied Jeff as he reached down to scratch O'Brien behind the ears.

"Yeah, seemed very preoccupied," said Cat thoughtfully.

"So, where do we go from here?" asked Jeff.

"I guess we just need to wait and see what the Garda discover. In the meantime, don't forget that you're meeting Ryan at the pub later. While you're there, try to get him to talk about the relationship between his father and Edward."

"Why are you so interested in that?"

"Didn't you notice that Edward appeared almost terrified of his father?"

"Actually, no I didn't. I was too busy trying to hold onto O'Brien to keep him from finishing him off," laughed Jeff at the thought of The O'Brien having to use anything other than his sheer size to restrain anyone.

With the mention of his name, The O'Brien was up from his bed by the stove and resting his head on the table between the two friends.

"There's our big fellow," cooed Cat in the baby voice that always set O'Brien's tail thumping.

"Looks like you have done a better job finding clues to this mystery than the Garda have in all this time," remarked Jeff as he stroked O'Brien's head.

Looking over at Cat, Jeff asked, "So what will you be doing while I'm out getting rat assed down the pub with your Ryan?

"Wait a minute. He's not my Ryan."

"I've known you for quite some time now Catherine Murphy and I can tell when you like the look of someone. And I can assure you being a man, I can tell when another man is attracted to a woman. Why do you think he invited me to the pub tonight?"

"Umm…maybe, just for a drink and some male companionship? I don't know."

"No. He is checking out the competition. He needs to find out exactly what our relationship is."

"You're crazy Jeff," laughed Cat punching Jeff playfully on the shoulder.

"But getting back to your original question, I'm going to enjoy a quiet night in and hopefully get some writing done. Just The O'Brien and me."

As he started out the door, Jeff smiled at the sight of Cat typing away on her laptop in front of the open fire with The O'Brien stretched out at her feet.

"I would say lock the door and don't let anyone in but I guess I needn't worry with your bodyguard standing guard over you," called Jeff as he began to close the door behind him.

With a wave of her hand, Cat called back, "Have fun and beware of the local brew and those wild Irish girls!"

Setting her laptop aside, Cat poured a glass of wine and pondered the recent events. Before long the warmth of the fire and the effect of the wine had Cat drifting off into a peaceful sleep.

Chapter 16

A peaceful sleep was anything but what Maureen was having across the lane. Dreams of her youthful days and the love she had shared with Edward Granville played over and over in her dreams. Those were the happiest days of her young life, until the old man had forced Edward into marrying the orphaned daughter of his millionaire best friend. Edward had explained that the estate needed money and by marrying Lillian not only would the manor survive but the survival of Ballysea would also be guaranteed.

The old man even had the audacity to tell Edward he could still keep Maureen as his 'little bit of fluff on the side.' Maureen still remembered the violent scene when Edward had suggested that very thing to her. It was a beautiful moonlit night as the two lovers walked the beach hand in hand. Taking her in his arms he told Maureen of his marriage plans and asked her to be his mistress.

No sooner were the words out of his mouth then Maureen nails raked his face and running from the beach she yelled back over her shoulder, "That's all of me you will ever have from this moment on."

Waking from her sleep, Maureen climbed out the bed she shared with her husband and wandered into the kitchen. Fixing a cup of tea, she began to wonder if the rumors were true. Even though she still resented Edward for being a coward and giving her up, she still could not believe that he would murder the mother of his child. If in fact, Marian was his child.

"I'm borrowing trouble," mused Maureen remembering her late mother's words for not worrying about things for which she had no control over.

Looking out her window toward Cat's cottage, Maureen sees the shadow of a man approaching Cat's cottage, 'Looks like Jeff is home early from the pub,' she thought.

As the lights of a passing car shone on the figure, Maureen recognizes Edward Granville raising his hand to knock on Cat's door.

"Now what's he up to?" whispers Maureen to herself as she slips into her shoes and pulls on her coat.

The sound of The O'Brien growling quickly wakes Cat from her peaceful sleep.

"What is it boy? Did Jeff forget his key?" sighed Cat as she made her way to the door.

Opening the door, she was surprised to be staring into the face of Edward Granville. Before she could say a word, Edward asked quietly, "Is it true? Is it Lillian?"

Sensing that she wasn't in any danger from the now obviously sober Edward, Cat asks, "Would you like to come in?"

"Is it safe?" asks Edward nodding in the direction of the still growling O'Brien.

"It is now," replied Cat as she pointed her hand to the floor to signal The O'Brien to sit and stay.

Walking into the now brightly lit kitchen, Cat put the kettle on and sat down at the table facing Edward.

"News certainly does travel fast around here," she remarked as she poured the tea and laid the milk and sugar on the table.

As he noisily stirred the sugar around in his tea cup Edward replied with a sigh, "I stopped in the pub and that's all that everyone is talking about. I don't remember that pub ever being so crowded. I guess death is good for business."

It was at that moment that Cat looked at Edward's face and realized that perhaps she and everyone else may have been wrong about Edward. This wasn't the expression of a man that thought this find might implicate him in a murder. This was the face of a man experiencing profound grief.

Reaching over and placing her hand over his, Cat said softly "I really can't tell you anymore than you probably already know. All we were told was that the remains were female and nothing more. I'm afraid we all will have to wait until the Garda finish their investigation."

"I know everyone blames me for Lillian. God knows I was a terrible husband but she was the mother of my child and I did love her in my own way. I swear to you that despite everything she put me through I would never have harmed her."

"But you did harm her little dog, didn't you Edward?" replied Cat as she continued to watch Edwards face.

"Boston? Why do you ask? I didn't care for the little beast but I'd never harm him. Marian loved that little dog too and despite what everyone thinks, I do love my daughter more than life itself."

Cat was confused now. If Edward was to be believed and he didn't kill the dog and had nothing to do with his wife's disappearance then who did? And what was he eluding to when he made the remark about what Lillian had put him through?

Before Cat had the chance to try to find out what Edward meant the sudden familiar thumping of O'Brien's tail announced the close presence of her neighbor. Opening the door Cat yelled out into the darkness, "Come on in Maureen. I know you are out there."

As Maureen sheepishly entered the cottage she said, "I saw Edward outside your house and after the incident at the manor the other day I wanted to be sure that you weren't in any danger."

"No trouble. Edward was just down the pub and heard the news so naturally he stopped by."

Edward was on his feet the moment Maureen entered the room. "How are you Maureen? It's been a long time. You're looking well."

"And you are looking much better than the last time I saw you drunk and flat on your back with himself here on top of you," replied Maureen with a hint of a smile playing around her full lips as she reached down to pat O'Brien's head.

"So, how did you know it was me outside?" asked Maureen.

Laughing Cat replied, "The O'Brien here has a certain way of wagging that tail of his when you come over every morning with his favorite treats. I'd know if you were within a mile of this place."

Now both Edward and Maureen joined in the laughter as the front door flew open and Jeff staggered in being helped by Ryan. "Looks like the real party is in here," slurred Jeff.

"I think you have had enough partying for one night Mr. Hunter. Can you guys manage to get him upstairs and out of his clothes and in his bed or should I just leave him where he falls?" asked Cat.

As both Granville brothers helped Jeff to his bed. Cat looked at Maureen and whispered, "Tomorrow, my dear friend, you can tell me the real story about you and Edward."

Once Jeff was settled in bed and the Granville's and Maureen finally left, Cat sat and tried to make sense of everything she had heard and observed this night and wondered what other surprises awaited her.

Chapter 17

Cat was still in her pajamas when the knock at the door came early the next morning. Assuming it to be Maureen, she unlocked the door and padding to the kitchen to start the coffee yelled, "Come on in. It's unlocked."

Still standing on Cat's doorstep and opening the door just a crack, Garda Burke, the younger of the two officers on the case, replied, "Sorry to bother you so early this morning Ms. Murphy. But we have some more details on the victim."

Reaching for the shawl she always kept hanging by the front door Cat covered herself and replied, "Won't you come in? I'm decent now. I thought you were my neighbor coming for her morning coffee."

Garda Burke slowly eased his way into the kitchen and removing his hat said, "I do apologize for disturbing you so early but I was just going off shift when I got the word and I figured beings you and the big fellow here made the discovery it was only right you should know."

Passing a freshly brewed mug of coffee over to the young Garda, Cat wondered what this urgent news was.

"Milk and sugar, Garda Burke?"

'Yes please and you can call me Mike if you like, everyone here in Ballysea does. My Da worked up at the manor and we lived in one of the crofts up there, so everyone in town has known me since before I was even born,"

Filling her cup with coffee, Cat sat facing Mike and said, "So what is this news?"

"Well, the pathologist isn't nearly half finished with all the tests but he did tell us that the remains are those of a juvenile girl."

"That rules out Lillian Granville then," replied Cat thoughtfully. "Well, thank goodness for that. I don't mind telling you that Edward Granville stopped by last night after hearing the news down at the pub and was distraught at the thought it could have been his wife. I truly believe he thinks his wife just left town and abandoned him and their daughter."

122

Scratching his head Mike replied, "Between you and me, I grew up with both Edward and Ryan and out of the two of them Edward was the most kind hearted."

"Really," mused Cat. "That does surprise me."

"I know that Edward has had problems with the drink and his temper of late but that all seemed to start after his marriage broke down. But believe me he doesn't have it in him to harm man or beast."

"So, now what Mike? I suppose that the investigation is looking into missing person cases now to try to identify the remains."

Solemnly Mike replied, "I assume you have met my uncle Jim Burke."

"Mr. Burke, The butcher? Yes, of course. I didn't realize he was your uncle. He's a lovely man and he and The O'Brien here have a special relationship. Don't you big fellow? He gives him treats every time we shop there," smiled Cat as she stroked the O'Brien's head.

"Have you heard about the tragic loss of his daughter, my cousin?"

"Oh no, do you think it could be her remains?"

Replying quietly, Mike explains that she is the only one to go missing in the area in the last 10 years. "You know, her body was never recovered from the sea and I'm thinking that the tide may have brought her in and somehow she washed into the cave and lay undiscovered all these years."

"Oh, how very tragic." replied Cat.

"Well, we should know for sure in a day or two after the dental records are checked. And if it is her, at least Uncle Jim will be able to see she has a proper Christian burial and he can visit her in the churchyard. He's a very devout man and that will mean so much to him."

"Then for your family's sake, I hope that it is she." replied Cat as she reached out to pat his hand.

"Thank you Ms. Murphy. I best be getting myself home. My wife will be wondering what's happened to me. And thank you again for the coffee. It's been a long night," said the young officer as he pushed his chair back from the table and headed for the door.

Walking with him to the door, Cat replied, "Thank you for taking the time to drop by and please pass on our best wishes to your family."

"Will do ma'am."

Slowly closing the door behind him, Cat poured another cup of coffee and reached for her cigarettes as Jeff came slowing creeping down the stairs.

"I thought I heard a voice. A male voice," remarked Jeff.

"Well, look who's up. Someone looks like death warmed over. How's your head this morning?

"Not very clear, I'm afraid. I don't think I can handle the dark stuff anymore."

"Well, I did warn you. The Guinness here is a lot stronger than what you get back in Annapolis."

"So, who dropped in this morning and caught you in your pajamas?"

"That was Garda Burke. He had some news for us."

"Which one is Garda Burke and what news?"

"He's the younger of the two officers and he wanted us to know that the remains are definitely not those of Lillian Granville."

"Wow, and they know this for sure?

"Yes. Apparently, they could determine right away that the remains were those of a juvenile girl and they think it may be the butcher James Burke's daughter who was drowned in the Bay a couple years back. Her body was never recovered. James Burke is actually Garda Burke's uncle so I felt really sorry for him."

"Well, that makes sense. Her body could have easily been forced into the cave at high tide and gotten trapped by all the brush when the tide went back out and then over time covered with sand."

O'Brien's loud tail thumping was followed by a light knock on the door announced the arrival of Maureen.

"Come in Maureen. The doors unlocked."

"Morning all. I saw that the Garda was here and I didn't want to intrude so I'm a bit late," replied Maureen as she deposited a plate of freshly made bacon butties on the table.

Slipping some bits of bacon to O'Brien, Maureen continued, "Sorry, but no scones this morning. I don't know what happened but I burnt them. First time I've done that since I was a child."

Catching the exchange of looks between the two women, Jeff declares, "I'm afraid my stomach isn't going to handle any food quite yet so I'm off to the shower and give you girls some time to catch up with the news."

Once Jeff had left the room, Cat told Maureen what Garda Burke had told her and watched as Maureen breathed a sigh of relieve.

"So, perhaps now you'd like to tell me about you and Edward Granville?" asked Cat as she reached for her cigarette pack.

Handing one over to Maureen, Cat continued, "Whatever you tell me will go no farther than this room."

"Oh Cat, I'm not worried about that. It's really ancient history and probably everyone in Ballysea with the exception of you and Jeff already know most of the story."

Cat sat quietly and let her friend talk of youthful love and betrayal.

When she had finished, Maureen said quietly, "Despite everything, I never really thought that Edward was capable of hurting Lillian knowing the effect it would have on Marian."

"I tend to agree with you now," replied Cat thoughtfully. Continuing Cat said, "You know Garda Burke said something rather strange this morning."

"What was that?"

"He said that out of the two brothers that Edward was not capable of hurting either man or beast, leaving me to assume that he felt quite differently about Ryan. I wonder what he observed while growing up so closely with them that made him think that."

"All three of them were very close as boys and Ryan was his father's favorite. You already know how I feel about the old man. Perhaps, Mike saw some of the old man's cruelty and spitefulness in Ryan at an early age."

"Perhaps, but he does seem very kind and gentle with Marian. He appears to really dote on the child.

"Yeah, well that," replied Maureen with a bit of a smirk on her face.

"What are you trying to tell me, Maureen?"

"Well, there was a lot of talk around town about the amount of time that Ryan and Lillian spent together when Edward was up in Dublin on manor business. They were seen out riding a lot and swimming over at the Cove on the far end of the manor. And then there is the resemblance between Ryan and the child," replied Maureen.

"Resemblance?"

"Yeah. Haven't you ever noticed? Lillian and Edward are both brown eyed and Marian's eyes are blue, just like Ryan's."

"Well, that doesn't really mean anything. Could be an inherited trait from some ancestor," replied Cat as her mind began to work overtime.

As Jeff returned to the kitchen to join the two friends, Maureen gave The O'Brien a final pat on the head and headed for the door, "Let me know if you hear anymore news. I'll see you later."

Noticing the pensive look on Cat's face, Jeff asks, "Why that look?"

Cat replied simply, "I have a feeling that things aren't as they seem."

Chapter 18

Ten days passed before Garda Burke knocked at Cat's door again with news of the remains.

"I'm afraid that the dental records have positively identified the remains of that of my cousin Flora," reported the young officer.

Cat rushed to fix the young man a cup of strong coffee as Jeff pulled out a chair for the young man.

Sliding the coffee in front of him, Cat quietly responded, "I am so sorry Mike. How is your uncle taking the news?"

"Well, as you can image, it has brought back the whole tragedy to him but at least now he has what you American's call closure. The remains are being released to the family today and he has scheduled a mass at St. Mary's next Saturday. She'll be laid to rest beside her mother immediately afterwards in the churchyard."

"Your poor uncle," sighed Cat.

"In a way, I think this will help him. My uncle is a very devout man and he just couldn't bear the fact that Flora had never been found and that she had been denied a proper Christian burial. Now at least he can feel she is at peace and resting beside her mother."

"I often passed your uncle on my daily walks on the beach and I would always see him standing up by the Point staring out into the bay but I had no idea of why until Cat told me of his loss after your last visit here. Please accept my condolences on the loss of your cousin and please let your uncle know that Cat and I will be at the service," said Jeff.

Draining the last of his coffee from his cup and getting to his feet, Mike responded, "Thank you both for everything you've said and done."

"We didn't do anything Mike. It was The O'Brien that found her and he's the one responsible for bringing your cousin home to rest," replied Jeff.

With the mention of his name, The O'Brien was on his feet and moving towards the door where Mike stood. Gently standing on his back paws, The O'Brien rested his paws on Mike's shoulders and just stared intently into his eyes before resting his big head on the grieving young officer's chest.

"Well I do swear he has just given me a hug," laughed Mike as he gently stroked the big dogs head.

As she closed the door behind Mike, Cat thought of how many times that The O'Brien had indeed shown compassion and brought closure to someone.

As she turned to face Jeff, she asks, "Now where do we go from here?"

"Well, I guess we start back at the beginning. We need to do a little more investigation. I think we need to go over the facts we already know and create a timeline of the events."

"Where do we start?" asked Jeff.

"Well, we know that your aunt was still alive when Lillian disappeared and also when Boston was killed and left on her doorstep, so that would put us sometime around Christmas last year," calculated Cat.

"Yes, that's about right," responded Jeff.

"I know that everyone suspects Edward but I have my doubts so I think we should start by trying to eliminate each person that might have cause, one at a time."

"Are you including your friend Maureen?" asked Jeff.

"Why, Maureen?"

"I'm a lawyer, remember Cat? It's obvious to anyone seeing the two of them together there was some type of relationship between them and in most cases if it isn't the spouse then a jealous lover is usually the obvious suspect."

"For goodness sakes Jeff, all that is ancient history. Maureen has been happily married for over 10 years and what happened between them when they were teenagers is hardly relevant now."

"Relevant or not, we still need to look at every possible suspect."

"Alright, I agree but first let's concentrate on Edward. I think I'll drop in on him up at the manor today and pass on Garda Burke's news. Maybe, I can get him to talk about the time that Lillian disappeared."

"Good idea. I can drive you up there later. Ryan promised me a tour of the manor grounds and maybe some grouse shooting."

The thumping of The O'Brien's tail announced the arrival of Maureen for her morning coffee.

Peeking under the cloth covered dish, Jeff was delighted to see his favorite warm scones and reaching onto the plate helped himself.

"They smell delicious. I see you didn't burn them this morning," smiled Jeff as he slathered on the creamy butter.

"Thank you. Yes, no distractions this morning. I purposely shut the kitchen curtains so I wouldn't be tempted to watch what was going on over here. I did, however, hear a car pull up earlier though," replied Maureen with one raised eyebrow.

Jeff couldn't help but laugh at the typically Irish way of trying to get the latest gossip, "Yes, that was Garda Burke. The remains have been positively identified through her dental records."

Maureen held her breath as Jeff continued, "They are the remains of his cousin Flora."

Letting out a sigh of relief, Maureen crossed herself and replied, "Poor Mr. Burke. I am so sorry. But at least he will have a proper place to visit her instead of staring out at the sea every day. It's all so sad. A parent should never have to bury their child."

The O'Brien was suddenly up and pacing at the door as Cat exclaimed, "Oh dear lord, I am so sorry big guy. With everyone coming and going this morning you haven't had your morning run."

As Cat prepared to take The O'Brien for his run on the beach, Maureen grabbed her arm and asked, "Mind if I join you? I could use a walk this morning."

"You girls go along," replied Jeff. I'll take care of the dishes and this last scone," as he snatched it up and took a huge bite.

Laughing Cat and Maureen were off at a run behind The O'Brien as he sprinted to the beach for his morning ritual of sea gull chasing.

About an hour into it the two friends plopped down on a large boulder with a panting O'Brien at their feet. Looking over at Cat, Maureen says, "In a way, I wish it had been Lillian and that she had died of natural causes. Perhaps then it might give Edward some peace. Don't get me wrong, I absolutely adore my husband and there is nothing between Edward and myself except memories. I would rather not think someone that I had cared so deeply for could commit such a horrible deed."

Slipping her arm around her friend's shoulder, Cat softly replies, "I understand exactly how you feel."

Maureen turns to look at Cat as she continued, "Have I ever told you about what brought me to Ballysea and about my husband?"

Maureen sat quietly and listened to Cat's tale of her love for her husband and his betrayal and when she had finished Cat said softly, "You see Maureen, I really do understand exactly how you feel."

Both women were on their feet and hugging each other when Jeff opened the door to let Cat know it was time to leave for the manor.

Chapter 19

The drive to the manor was anything but peaceful. Jeff had decided the moment they left Ballysea that he needed to listen to some hard rocking head banger music on the car stereo. By the time they reached the tree lined drive to the manor, Cat had a throbbing headache and was about to lose her mind.

Reaching over and switching off the radio brought Jeff's bobbing head to a dead stop.

"What did you do that for? I was just getting into it."

"You've been getting into it the whole way up here and I need a few minutes at least to get my thoughts together on how I approach the subject with Edward," replied Cat.

"Alright! Alright!" replied a petulant Jeff.

"I've got to somehow get him to talk about the evening that Lillian disappeared."

Scratching his head Jeff replied, "I would have thought that would be the easy part. Once you tell him that the remains have been identified as Flora Burke, tell him how sorry you are for everything he is going through. And how it must bring back memories of the last time he saw his wife. With any luck that should get him talking. If not then you'll need to use your secret weapon."

Looking confused Cat responded, "Umm...what secret weapon?"

Jeff pointed to the now sleeping O'Brien in the back seat and says, "Just say, don't make me put my vicious dog on you again."

With that, the two friends took one look at the peacefully sleeping O'Brien and burst out laughing.

The cloud of dust, signaled their arrival at the manor before the car had even turned the last bend. Ryan was waiting for them as Jeff parked the car and Cat and The O'Brien piled out.

"Hey Cat. How are you? I wasn't expecting you today. I was going to show Jeff around the grounds and do a little shooting but you're more than welcome to join us."

"Hi Ryan. I needed to get out of the house for awhile so I just came along for the ride and if it's alright with you let The O'Brien have a good run over your fields. Thought I'd have a word with Edward first thought if he's about," replied Cat.

"Sure, let him run as long as he doesn't bother the sheep. Edward was in the library the last I saw him. Is there anything that I should know?

Cat watched his face intently as she responded, "Garda Burke stopped by the cottage earlier. The remains in the cave were those of his cousin Flora."

"Oh, I am sorry to hear that. Terrible to lose a child like that," replied Ryan as he turned away and called over his shoulder, "You coming Jeff? Those birds won't wait for us forever."

As Jeff trailed along behind Ryan toward the out buildings, Cat thought, 'He didn't seem a bit surprised that it wasn't Lillian. I have a feeling that Ryan knows a lot more about Lillian's disappearance than he would like anyone to know.'

Reaching down and clipping on O'Brien's lead, Cat whispered, "This is more for your safety then theirs big guy. Someone around here obviously isn't fond of dogs."

Cat's knock on the door was answered promptly by Mrs. O'Malley. Wiping her hands on her apron, she asked, "May I help you?"

"Hello. I'm Cat Murphy. Is Edward at home?"

Looking her and The O'Brien up and down, the gray haired, rotund housekeeper turned her back and heading back toward the kitchen yelled, "Mr. Edward! There's a lady at the door asking for you and she's brought her beastie with her again."

With that, Cat heard a door open and footsteps hurrying down the hall.

"Hi Cat. It's good to see you! And how's The O'Brien today? In a friendly mood, I hope," laughed Edward.

This was the first time that Cat had actually seen Edward smile and she suddenly understood what Maureen must have seen in him.

"I'm forgetting my manners. Come on in. Would you like some tea?" asked Edward.

"I'd love some," replied Cat as Edward led her into a sumptuous sitting room.

"I'll be right back soon as I find Mrs. O'Malley. Please make yourself comfortable."

Cat wandered around the room looking at the furnishing and art work and wondered who decorated the room. It was obviously a woman. But was it Edward's late mother or his wife? Moving to the center of the room, she stopped in front of the massive fireplace and stared up at the portrait that hung above it. The young woman in the portrait was ethereal with luminous skin and wide doe like brown eyes and short wispy brown hair. She wore a simple empire style white gown and around her neck she wore the biggest and most beautiful sapphire necklace that Cat had ever seen.

Turning at the sound of rattling cups, Cat smiled as she watched Edward gingerly carrying the heavily laden tray into the sitting room.

"Hopefully, I haven't wrecked the presentation. Mrs. O'Malley said she wasn't about to carry a tray full of sandwiches anywhere around your beastie," laughed Edward.

"I don't think she would have had anything to worry about," giggled Cat as she pointed to The O'Brien happily rolling about on the massive sheepskin rug in front of the fireplace.

Pouring Cat a cup of tea, Edward said wistfully, "I saw you looking at the portrait. It was painted of Lillian when she was a few months pregnant with Marian."

Being very careful to refer to Lillian in the present tense Cat replied, "She is very beautiful."

"Thank you," replied Edward.

"And this room. It is absolutely stunning. Did your wife decorate it?"

"Actually, this was my mother's room. This was her special sanctuary. My father never comes in here. The decor is too feminine for his tastes but I love it," replied Edward.

"So what brings you here today? Looking for Ryan? If so, I'm afraid that you've just missed him. He is out shooting today."

"No. I actually came to see you and I know that Ryan is shooting. Jeff has gone with him. I have news about the remains that The O'Brien discovered."

Edward dropped his cup, spilling tea all over the antique Chippendale table and splashing Cat. "I'm so sorry," sputtered Edward as he mopped at Cat's lap with his napkin.

Raising her eyebrow, Cat took the napkin from his hand and smiled, "No harm done."

Cat quickly added, "Edward, it wasn't your wife. It was Flora Burke."

"Oh thank god! Then she must have just run away. I was so afraid that I might have driven her to commit suicide," exclaimed Edward as he covered his face with his hands.

"Suicide? Why would you think that she might do that?" questioned Cat.

Quickly changing the subject, Edward regained his composure and continued, "How thoughtless of me to think of my own troubles first. Poor Mr. Burke. How is he taking it?"

"I haven't actually spoken to him but his nephew, the younger of two investigating Garda, says he is actually doing quite well. He is content now that Flora will have a Christian burial and can lie beside her mother in the churchyard."

"I am glad. Have they announced the time for the funeral service?"

"It will be Saturday but I'm not sure of the time."

A mechanical buzzing noise announced the entrance at the doorway of the elder Lord Granville. "What's this about a funeral? Hope it isn't mine that you are planning."

With the sound of the wheelchair, The O'Brien was immediately up on his feet and beside his mistress and staring intently at the old man's face.

It was then that Cat remembered what James Burke had told her on her first day in Ballysea about wolfhounds searching a man's face for signs of deceit. If this old Irish folk tale was true than The O'Brien was certainly searching for something in the old man's face.

"Father, you remember Ms. Murphy from the Open Day. She stopped by to tell me the remains that were found in the sea cave were Jim Burke's daughter, Flora."

The old man merely grunted and shaking his cane at The O'Brien, he reversed his wheelchair and leaving the room yelled, "Please remove the beast from my home. I can't abide dogs indoors."

"Sorry about that big fellow," muttered an embarrassed Edward as he stroked O'Brien's head. "Maybe, I can make it up to you with a few of these nice meat sandwiches and a romp in the meadow."

Feeling his discomfort, Cat quickly replied, "I've an idea. How about a picnic in the meadow?"

Edward broke into a broad smile and soon the three of them were off across the drive dragging Marian's toy wagon laden with the tea service and a blanket behind them. Turning to look back at the manor, Cat saw the face of the old Lord staring back from a window.

Cat felt suddenly very cold and consumed by a feeling of dread.

Chapter 20

Once they had reached the meadow, Cat unclipped The O'Brien's lead and let him run free. Cat always marveled at how graceful the big animal was when he was in full stride. It was amazing how much ground he could cover with those long strides. Before she knew it, O'Brien had crossed the meadow and was investigating the wooded area beyond.

Shielding her eyes from the bright sun, she turned to watch Edward.

"He's truly magnificent, isn't he? When mother was alive, Ryan and I always had pet dogs. After she died, father sold them off to some travelers that were passing through. Said we had ruined them and if they weren't good for retrieving the birds he shot then they weren't worth the cost of the food we fed them."

As Cat sat watching The O'Brien explore, she heard the echo of gun fire.

Jumping to her feet she quickly whistled for The O'Brien to return to her side. Within minutes he was there.

Edward reached into the wagon and lifting a meat filled sandwich gingerly held it out to the waiting O'Brien.

Cat smiled as O'Brien looked at the sandwich and licking his lips looked over to her for permission to take the treat from Edward. Seeing the hurt and confusion on Edward's face, Cat quickly explained, "O'Brien doesn't take food from strangers unless he is told that it is OK."

Giving The O'Brien the hand signal he had been taught, Cat smiled up at Edward and said, "He'll take it from you now."

Offering the sandwich to O'Brien again, Edward was delighted when the big dog gently took the treat from his fingers.

"He's what we call soft-mouthed," said Edward quietly as he reached to hand O'Brien another sandwich.

"Soft-mouthed?"

Edward explained, "If a dog is soft mouthed it means they will carry game in their mouth without biting into it. It's a really sought after trait in hunting dogs. You don't want to have you dinner chewed up before you can get it to the table. You can usually tell if a dog will be soft mouthed when they are a pup by the way they accept food from your hand."

As Cat sat watching Edward's gentle interaction with The O'Brien, she became more and more convinced that Maureen and the towns' people had been wrong about Edward's involvement in the killing of Boston.

At the sound of another shotgun report, Cat reached over and clipped the lead onto O'Brien's collar.

"Sorry, big fellow but those guns seem like they are getting closer and I'm not sure how good of a shot our Jeff is. We don't want to be in his line of fire."

"Perhaps, we should be getting back," said Edward as he rose to his feet and offered Cat a hand up.

Once on her feet, Cat found herself staring directly into Edward's warm brown eyes and summoning up the courage asked, "Edward, why did you say you were afraid that Lillian may have taken her own life?"

Letting go of Cat's hand and taking a step back Edward replied, "It is a very long story Cat. As I told you that night at your cottage, I wasn't a very good husband."

Seeing the hurt expression in Edward's eyes, Cat reached for his hand and confided, "We all have regrets about our failed relationships."

"Well, your relationship with Jeff seems happy enough," replied Edward.

"My relationship with Jeff?"

"Yeah, you two seem happy and it's obvious that he adores you," replied Edward.

"That's because we are only best friends and not in a relationship, Edward. Lord, if I had to put up with Jeff's idiosyncrasies or he with mine on a permanent basis we may very well both end up in prison," laughed Cat as she wondered if everyone in Ballysea thought that she and Jeff were a couple.

Pulling the wagon along behind him as they began the trek back to the manor, Edward looked down at Cat and said, "Thanks for coming all the way out here to give me the news about Flora and thanks for suggesting this picnic. I have really enjoyed the afternoon."

As they approached the front door of the manor, Jeff and Ryan came strolling out of the barn.

Edward was the first to greet them, "How many did you bag?"

Ryan replied, "We managed to bag ten, so father will be pleased that he can have his favorite dinner a couple times this week. We've already dropped them off to Mrs. O'Malley in the kitchen."

"How was the shooting, Jeff," asked Cat.

"The shooting went well. It was just finding the birds after we had shot them that took so much time."

Edward replied, "You should have had The O'Brien with you. I bet that he would make a great gun dog."

Cat reached down to rub behind O'Brien's ears as he leaned against her and wondered if it was her imagination or if The O'Brien was really acting protective every time Ryan appeared.

Switching her attention to Edward, she said, "Thank you for a lovely afternoon. Will we see you Saturday at the funeral?"

"Yes, I imagine Ryan and I will both be there representing the family. Father can't manage the steps with his wheelchair."

Settling The O'Brien in the back seat before climbing into the passenger seat, Cat and Jeff waved goodbye to the Granville's and began the short drive back to Ballysea.

Before they had even left the estate, Cat turned to Jeff and stated, "There is evil in that house."

Chapter 21

The sky had turned gray and brooding as they left the estate and began their drive back to Ballysea. As they drove, Cat shared with Jeff what she had learned during her visit with Edward at the manor.

"From what you have said, the old man sounds like a real tyrant. Oddly enough though, Ryan seems very fond of him and it's obvious the old man favors the younger of the two brothers. Perhaps that might account for Edward's resentment towards both of them," remarked Jeff.

"Really, you think Edward resents Ryan? I didn't pick up on that from any of my conversations with him," mused Cat.

"Well, maybe you are looking at Edward through the proverbial rose tinted glasses?" replied Jeff giving Cat a sideways glance.

"And what do you mean by that?"

"Honestly Cat, have you forgotten that I'm not only a lawyer but a man too? I can tell when a man is interested in you. And if I'm not mistaken, you are sympathetic to him too."

"Really Jeff, I think I recall you saying the same thing about me and his brother. But you are right about one thing. I am sympathetic to Edward. From what I can tell, he has had a miserable life ever since his mother passed and having a marriage to someone he barely knew forced upon him, well it's just beyond me how a father can be so heartless to his own son."

"What makes you think that his life was so miserable? Ryan seems well enough adjusted and he hasn't hinted their childhood was anything other than happy with the exception of the normal trauma of losing their mother."

As they pulled up in front of Cat's cottage, Cat tells Jeff about the old man selling the boys' pet dogs immediately after their mother's funeral."

Rubbing his chin, Jeff replies, "Well, that was a bit cold."

As she helped The O'Brien out of his cramped quarters in the back seat, Cat replied, "Cold? It's just plain cruel. Furthermore, I didn't appreciate the menacing way he treated The O'Brien."

"Really Cat, aren't you overreacting a bit now. He's an old man in a wheelchair. How could he possibly do anything to harm The O'Brien?"

"I don't know, Jeff. But I just don't trust that man and I can assure you that after today I will be keeping a much closer eye on O'Brien."

The soft mist had turned to rain as they entered the cottage. Cat went straight into the kitchen to put the kettle on while Jeff added some coals to the fire.

"The day has sure turned gray and damp. I'll get this fire banked for the evening before I change out of these muddy clothes and shower. Is there anything in the refrigerator to make a sandwich with?" yelled Jeff from the parlor.

"Not really. We finished off the last of the gammon at breakfast this morning and we're out of bread," replied Cat.

"Well, looks like we'll have to go down to the pub for a meal," replied Jeff faking disappointment as he climbed the stairs.

Laughing Cat replied, "Don't sound so disappointed. I know you'd rather have a hot meal and a cold pint at the pub than a cold sandwich and a hot tea here with me. I won't even mention the company of a certain young lady that I have noticed you checking out."

With the mention of food, The O'Brien began prancing around the table and making the low groaning noises that never failed to bring a smile to Cat's face.

Ruffling his hair, Cat said, "My goodness, O'Brien. If anyone could hear you, they would swear I had a big pig in here. Don't worry big guy. You're going with us and I'm sure we can find something on the menu that will suit your fancy." Cat loved that well behaved dogs were always welcome to accompany their owners at the local pubs.

The rain had finally stopped but the clouds covering the moon made it pitch dark as the two friends with The O'Brien at their side started down the lane toward the pub that sat opposite the small fishing harbor. Cat loved the warmth of the old building that housed the pub. With its two large lead pane bow windows facing out across the bay it was a perfect place to sit on clear nights and watch the rose and yellow sunsets. Tonight was definitely not one of those nights.

Hearing the sound of a car behind them, they moved off the narrow lane onto the ridge that separated the lane from the beach. As the engine noise grew louder, O'Brien suddenly pulled back hard on his lead jerking Cat around. Cat turned her head just in time to see the car barreling down on them. In a split second, Cat pushed Jeff and then jumped dragging The O'Brien with her over the ridge and onto the beach below.

"Jesus, what just happened? Did you see anything?" yelled Jeff as he was up on his feet and climbing back up on the ridge hoping to get a glimpse of the fleeing car.

Checking to see that The O'Brien hadn't been injured in the fall, Cat yelled back, "When I turned back the car was on the wrong side of the road and coming right at us. Their lights were off so I couldn't make out much about the driver or the car. All I can say for sure is that it was a dark late model sedan."

"We're almost at the pub so let's go there and call the Garda. We can at least get something to eat while we wait for them. I have a feeling this is going to be another long night."

Brushing the sand from her jeans, Cat knelt down and wrapping her arms around The O'Brien whispered, "Looks like you saved me again. If you hadn't tugged at your leash like that I would've never seen that car and things could have turned out much differently."

Cat didn't stop shaking until they reached the well lite safety of the pub. Finding a table close to the open fire, Jeff put a call in to the Garda in Sligo and then went to the bar returning with two pints and a menu.

"It'll be awhile before they get here so we still have time to eat. I told them that we were calling from

162

the pub so I'm sure they'll stop here first. Frankly, after what happened tonight I won't mind having the police bring me home for once," stated Jeff.

Cat had all but lost her appetite but ordered a burger for herself and three for The O'Brien while Jeff ordered his usual fish and chips.

They had barely started their meal when Garda Mike Burke came strolling through the front door and pulled up a chair and sat at their table.

"That was fast. We weren't expecting you for at least another 20 minutes or longer," remarked Jeff between shoveling malt vinegar laden chips into his mouth.

"I'm actually off duty on bereavement leave this week but I heard the call so I thought I might as well come down for a pint and keep you company until someone from the station shows up," replied Mike.

"Let me get you that pint and Cat can fill you in on what happened. The only thing I saw was the sand on the beach where I landed face down," volunteered Jeff as he headed back to the bar.

After listening intently to Cat's description of the incident Mike said, "Sorry, but I have to ask. Have either of you made any enemies since you have been over here?"

Looking at each other and finally nodding agreement, they both began in turns to tell Mike about what Cat had found in her garden and their amateur investigation into Lillian Granville's disappearance.

"That's all well and good, but you really should leave this to the Garda," replied Mike rather sternly.

It was at that very moment that Jeff decided to drop a time bomb, as he loudly declared, "After the events of this evening, I am now more than ever convinced that there has been at least one murder that has gone unsolved and tomorrow I am going to arrange to have my aunt's remains exhumed and a thorough examination performed. Her death so close to Lillian's disappearance and her dog's brutal killing is just too much of a coincidence."

Cat sat quietly starring at her closest friend and wondered what exactly he was playing at. He had deliberately made his declaration loud enough for everyone in the pub to clearly hear.

They just finished their meal when the Garda arrived from the station and after greeting Mike and offering their condolences for his loss; they took Cat's statement and escorted them home.

Saying good night at the door, Mike Burke said, "I'm sure it was someone that had too much to drink but just in case, please make sure you keep your doors and windows locked until we get to the bottom of this."

As Jeff closed and locked the door behind Garda Burke, Cat reached down and spoke seriously to The O'Brien, "Looks like we might be sleeping with one eye open tonight big fellow."

No sooner were the words out of her mouth than The O'Brien walked over to the door and laid down in front of it.

Smiling Jeff said, "Well, looks like someone is planning on sleeping with both eyes closed. One thing for sure, if anyone gets near that door we'll know it in a hurry."

Dragging his dog bed over to the door, Cat patted O'Brien's big head and said, "If you must sleep in front of the door you might as well be comfortable. I won't have the hero of the night sleeping on the cold slate floor."

"Why don't you sleep upstairs tonight? Get a good night's rest. I feel like sitting up for awhile and I'll sleep on the sofa," said Jeff as he dropped down on the sofa.

"If you don't mind, I'll join you for awhile."

Patting the sofa cushion, Jeff slid over and made room for Cat and slipping a brotherly arm around her shoulder said, "Things will look better in the light of morning."

Cat wondered if the light of a new day would erase the feeling of dread that now consumed her.

Chapter 22

It was almost midnight before Cat finally made her way up the stairs, leaving Jeff snoring in front of the fire. Exhausted from the events of the day, sleep eluded Cat as she tossed and turned into the early hours of the morning. Finally exasperated, Cat climbed out of bed and silently crept downstairs. As soon as her feet hit the floor, Cat heard the unmistakable thumping of The O'Brien's tail.

The clock on the kitchen wall read 6"00 am and crossing to the door, Cat stroked O'Brien's head and whisper, "Good morning sweetie. Looks like you didn't have a very good night's sleep either."

Yawning, Cat made her way to the stove and started the coffee.

"Soon as I get a cup of coffee, I'll take you out for your morning walk," promised Cat as The O'Brien yawned then waited patiently at the door. Finally, with her cup of steaming coffee in her hand Cat padded over to the door.

Pulling the door open, Cat almost knocked over Maureen who was just raising her hand to knock on the door.

"Sorry for coming over so early but I saw the Garda here again last night. Have they discovered anything new?"

"Nothing new about Lillian's disappearance but someone did try to murder us last night," replied Cat.

"What? Oh my god Cat. What happened?"

"Walk with me and I'll tell you all about it," replied Cat slipping her arm through Maureen's.

Arm and arm, the two friends with The O'Brien keeping guard slowly walked down the path to the beach. As she watched The O'Brien sniffing the air, Cat realized that the events of the previous evening had made a profound effect on her four legged bodyguard. The O'Brien didn't wander as usual this morning but stayed close to her side in full protection mode.

After telling Maureen about the near miss, she said, "We have gotten close to finding out something."

"But what, Cat?"

"I'm not sure, Maureen. One thing I do know is that the answer lies at the manor. I just have to find a way to look around up there without arousing any suspicion," replied Cat as they started the climb back to her cottage for a much needed second coffee and cigarette.

Jeff was awake and had more coffee brewing when The O'Brien pushed the door open with his nose followed in by Cat and Maureen.

"Good thing our friend from last night didn't decide to make an early morning visit. You not only left the door unlocked but half open."

Maureen quickly apologized, "Sorry Jeff. That was my fault. I startled Cat as she was just taking O'Brien for his walk."

"That's alright. No harm done. I was awake anyway and have been keeping a watchful eye out the window on you guys. I take it Cat told you about what happened last night," replied Jeff.

"She did. Frankly, I don't know what to think. Nothing like this has ever happened around here."

"There's something else you should know. I have decided to have my aunt exhumed and I announced it rather loudly at the pub last night so I'm sure at least half of Ballysea knows by now. I'm not completely satisfied that her sudden death was natural."

Maureen's look of shock left nothing to the imagination as she gasped, "You actually think that someone killed her?"

"I think it's a strong possibility. Perhaps she knew more than what was good for her."

Settling back in his chair, Jeff continued," Did my aunt have any regular visitors after Lillian disappeared?"

"Well, yes. Now that you mention it. Ryan used to stop by with Marian almost weekly and bring her groceries and supplies," replied Maureen.

Cat and Jeff exchanged meaningful glances as Cat replied, "More than ever, I am sure the answers we seek are at the manor. I just need a good excuse to get up there and have a good look around."

It wasn't long before Cat got the opportunity to do just that.

Chapter 23

That excuse came soon enough as she and Jeff were leaving Flora Burke's funeral on Saturday. Stepping out into the sunshine from the dimly lit church, Edward and Ryan stood waiting by the door for Cat and Jeff.

"Good Morning Cat. I was hoping to run into you here."

"Good Morning Edward. How are you?"

"As well as can be expected, I suppose. I feel so sorry for the Burke family but at least they have closure and they know where Flora is. Anyway, I was just wondering if you'd like to go riding tomorrow. You'd be doing me a favor. The horses need the exercise and so do I," laughed Edward as he patted a non-existent stomach.

"I'd be delighted. I haven't ridden since I left the States but I did bring my boots with me hoping to get some riding in while I was here. Around 10:00?"

"Perfect. See you then," replied Edward as he climbed into his Land Rover. Waving goodbye he headed out of town towards the manor.

Throwing his arm around Jeff's shoulder, Ryan asked, "Fancy a drink at the pub?"

Looking over at Cat, who had now been joined by Maureen and her husband Liam, Jeff asked, "You want to join us Cat?"

"No thanks. You two go along and enjoy yourselves. I want to get home to The O'Brien."

Noticing the concerned look on Jeff's face, Maureen winked at Cat and quickly said," Liam and I will see her home and then I'll be over for some girl talk."

As they walked up the hill, Maureen looked back as the two men entered the pub laughing. "Now, those two together look like trouble looking for a place to happen."

Seeing the two friends safely in the cottage, Liam said his goodbyes and headed home to take the children into town for a bag of penny candy each as a reward for doing their chores all week.

The O'Brien was waiting for them at the door, as the two friends entered.

"It amazes me that he always knows when we are coming before we even get close to the door," said Maureen reaching down to pat his head.

Laughing Cat pointed to the closed window curtain at the front of the house," Yes, he is amazing but I think if you feel those curtains you'll find that there are wet spots from his nose where he has been opening them to look out."

Handing a treat to The O'Brien, Cat looks over at Maureen and asks, "What did you mean with that trouble looking for a place to happen comment?"

"I was talking about Ryan, not Jeff."

"So, why is he trouble?"

"He's nice and polite and all that but has a bit of a reputation of being a little too free with the ladies, especially the married ones, if you know what I mean."

"You sound like you're speaking from experience," said Cat watching her friend's face.

"Yeah, he tried it on with me. For some reason, he seems to have this uncontrollable need to have anything that belongs to his older brother. It wasn't long after Edward and I broke up that he was beating a path to my front door. I had his number right away though. He never knew I was alive until Edward and I got together then he was tagging along with us every chance he got. It got worse after Edward's engagement was announced. It was like he wanted to possess what Edward wanted but couldn't have. He even asked me to marry him."

Reaching for and uncorking a bottle, Cat poured them each a glass of white wine and toasting her best friend said," Slainte."

Maureen replied, "Slainte. But what are we drinking to?"

"We are drinking to your lucky escape from being in that strange family and your excellent choice in husbands. Here's to you and Liam," replied Cat as she clinked glasses with her friend.

"Thanks Cat. You know the thought of living under the same roof as the old Lord Granville as my father-in-law really creeped me out even back then. He's always been a strange one. First his wife dying with that mysterious illness that none of the local doctors could seem to diagnose and then the disappearance of Lillian. It just wouldn't make any woman in her right mind want to be a member of that family."

"The way Edward talked I got the impression his mother died of cancer or some other lingering illness,'" remarked Cat.

"Yeah, it was a long illness but I never heard what the actual cause of death was and the strangest thing was he had her cremated immediately after she died."

"I would have thought with her position in the community that there would have been a large funeral and she would have been buried in the family crypt at the church," replied Cat thoughtfully.

"Everyone thought that but with so many in the town depending on their jobs at the manor for their income, no one said anything. I don't mind telling you though there was a lot of whispered speculation at the time."

"I'm sure," was all that Cat replied as her mind flashed back to the evil expression on the old Lord's face as he watched Edward and her leave for their picnic.

Swirling her wine around in her glass Maureen asked, "So what's with you and Edward?"

"Nothing. Why?"

"Sorry Cat but I couldn't help but overhear Edward invite you to go riding with him tomorrow. You're taking Jeff with you aren't you?"

"Jeff wouldn't know one end of a horse from the other so probably not besides I think he mentioned something about going shooting with Ryan tomorrow and I volunteered The O'Brien to go with them and retrieve."

"Well, you be very careful. I don't like the idea of you going up to the manor by yourself," replied Maureen.

"I won't be alone. I'll be with Edward. You still don't suspect him of anything, do you?"

"No I honestly don't, but I don't think that incident with the car was just someone driving over the limit either."

Cat felt the chill starting at the bottom of her spine and traveling up her back as she shivered, "Feels like someone just walked across my grave."

Chapter 24

The next morning dawned bright but a little chilly as Cat dug out her riding clothes and prepared for her ride with Edward.

Jeff couldn't help but notice that the once loose fitting outfit now clung to all the right curves as he waited for Cat and The O'Brien to get into the car for the drive to the manor.

"So are my two best guys ready to bring home dinner for tonight," asked Cat as they started out of town towards the manor.

"Sure are. Aren't we big guy?" asked Jeff as he looked through the rear view window at The O'Brien. The only reply from the back was a grunt from a rather indifferent O'Brien as he stared out the back window at the passing countryside.

As they pull up to the manor, Ryan and Edward were just exiting the barn, "Looks like we arrived at the perfect time. At least now, we won't have to go into the manor."

"So, that place gives you the creeps too, huh?" asked Cat as she looked toward the manor door shielding her eyes from the bright sun.

"Not so much the manor, but the old Lord. There's just something about him that makes the hairs on the back of my neck stand up."

Opening the car door for Cat, Edward says, "Morning Cat. I see you found your riding clothes."

"Yes and by some miracle they still fit despite all those lovely scones that Maureen tempts me with every morning," laughed Cat as she pulled open the back door to let The O'Brien out.

True to his nature, Ryan couldn't help looking Cat up and down until Jeff shaking his head says, "Are we ready for that shoot?"

Tearing his eyes away from Cat's shapely bottom, Ryan replies, "Sure, let's go bag us some birds."

Leaning down, Cat takes The O'Brien's head in her hands and says, "You go with Jeff and help him find those birds OK? I'm going riding with Edward and I'll be fine."

With a wave of her hand in Jeff's direction, The O'Brien was off across the drive following the two men as Cat and Edward made their way to the stable. Catching up to Jeff, he nudges him and stops and looks back to the stable and takes two steps back in the direction that Cat has disappeared.

Walking back to him Jeff says, "Come on big guy, you heard what she said. She'll be fine. She's with Edward." Hesitating, O'Brien finally trails off behind them but not without turning and looking back until they had reached the meadow and the stable was out of sight.

The inside of the stable smelled of sweet hay as Edward introduced Cat to the horses that she could pick from for her ride.

"If you haven't ridden for a while, I would suggest Molly here. She's gentle and sure-footed but can still give you a good gallop if that's what you want. I'll be riding Trooper over here. He hasn't been exercised in a while so I have a feeling that he's going to be ready for a good run."

The whizzing sound of the motorized wheelchair as it approached the stable door soon interrupted their conversation as the elder Lord Granville entered the stable.

"Good Morning Ms. Murphy. Nice to see you again," smiled the old man before continuing. "Edward, I hate to interrupt your ride, but can you pop over to my study for a moment so we can discuss the County Livestock Show and you can sign the papers for me?"

"Sure father. I'll be back in a moment Cat. Have a look around and get to know Molly."

Cat watched as the father and son entered the manor and closed the door behind them.

"Might as well get you saddled up Molly," said Cat as she patted the big chestnuts neck and headed for one of the two doors on either side of the stable.

"Well, one of these has to be the tack room," she said out loud as she pushed the door open.

She had no sooner entered the room when she heard footsteps behind her and felt the barrel of a gun in her back.

"I see you have found my car. I only drive it on very special occasions, like very dark nights," whispered the voice from behind her as her hands were wrenched back and secured with tape.

Turning her around to face him, he quickly tapes her mouth and drags her into the dark sedan.

"We're going for a little ride. You are so curious about where Lillian went then maybe it's time to show you."

Driving out away from the stable, Cat could hear the sound of gunfire fading away in the distance as old Lord Granville drove through a small wooded area to a part of the estate that she hadn't seen.

"These my dear are Bog fields. Have you ever heard the story of the Bog Man? He was an Irish king that was sacrificed and thrown into one of these peat bogs. His mummified remains were finally found centuries later. Would you believe it, his skin was still intact. Wonder if Lillian's is," snickered the old man.

Across the meadow, Ryan watching The O'Brien says, "Hey Jeff, I thought Cat said O'Brien was good at retrieving. Looks like he's more interested in something over in the woods then in finding our birds."

A sudden flash of light reflected off of the car mirror as it entered the wooded area had indeed attracted The O'Brien's attention and sensing trouble he began furiously barking at the two men before taking off across the fields toward the woods.

"Now what's he going on about," asked Ryan laughing.

Hesitating for just a moment Jeff yelled, "Cat's in trouble," as both men start running after O'Brien."

Dragging her from the car and pushing her to the edge of the bog, the old Lord says, "Nasty way to go or so I would think. You know, it was a shame about Lillian but if she hadn't played around with Ryan and planned on running away with him then she would still be here today and playing the part of the grand Lady of the Manor. But no, she had to try to take my favorite son and his child, my only grandchild, away from me. No one pays much attention to an old man in a wheelchair so even after I regained the use of my legs I didn't let on. You see, I overheard them planning to leave while Edward was away in Dublin and I just couldn't have that. It was an easy task to get her to leave the house while Ryan was in town and Edward in Dublin by using a note that Ryan had left earlier in the week for Edward saying 'Meet me in the stable' Once there, a good knock on the head made it easy to get her here. After disposing of her body it was a simple manner to just take the suitcase she had already conveniently packed and dispose of it over the cliff top after weighing it down. That stupid little dog must have gotten out of the manor and followed the scent to where I tossed the suitcase, so as soon as I had the chance, then I got rid of him too."

The old man was so consumed with his ranting that he didn't hear The O'Brien followed by Ryan and Jeff approaching.

"Well now you know. You have solved the mystery. For whatever good it will do you now," sneered the old man as he prepared to push a near fainting Cat into the marshy bog.

The last thing Cat saw out of the corner of her eye before she fainted was a flash of gray as the full power of the 200 pound wolfhound made impact with her captor sending him flying into the bog. Dragging Cat by her riding jacket away from the edge of the bog, The O'Brien dropped to her side as Jeff and Ryan tried desperately to get the old man out of the bog.

Leaning out the barrel of his shotgun, Ryan yelled, "Grab on father. I'll pull you out."

Shaking his head, the old man looks at his son and said, "I couldn't let her take you and Marian away. I knew about your affair and that you were Marian's father."

"What are you talking about? Come on father. You have to help us."

The old man replied, "No. Ask the girl. This is the way it has to be." These were his last words as a sucking noise was heard and the old man's head disappeared.

Pulling the tape from her mouth as he helped Cat to her feet, Ryan asks, "Where's my brother? Where's Edward?"

"After you left, your father called him back into the manor to sign some papers and Edward told me to wait in the barn."

The O'Brien was first to leave as the three piled into the sedan and headed back to the manor. On the short drive back, Cat told Ryan everything his father said before ending up in the bog. Finding Edward unconscious on the floor heavily sedated with The O'Brien already at his side, Ryan immediately called for an ambulance and the Garda.

Dropping down beside his brother, Ryan looks on as Cat feels for a pulse in Edward's neck.

"Is he going to make it Cat?"

"I don't know Ryan. I just hope that ambulance gets here in a hurry."

"This is all my fault. If I had been a good brother and stayed away from Lillian, she and father would still be alive, Marian would still have her mother and Edward would not be lying here now," moaned Ryan as he began to pace up and down the room.

It was only a half hour before the ambulance from Sligo arrived but it felt like a lifetime to Cat as she cradled Edward's head in her lap.

Chapter 25

The doctors at the hospital confirmed that Edward had indeed been drugged but were unable to tell the extent of any permanent damage until he woke from the drug induced coma. Consumed with guilt, Ryan rarely left his brother's bedside.

Finally, on the morning of the second day, Edward opened his eyes to find Cat dozing by the side of his bed holding Ryan's hand.

Looking over at Cat, Edward slurred, "Where am I?"

Leaning over the bed as she stroked the side of his face Cat whispered, "Welcome back to the world of the living. We were afraid we might lose you."

Directing his attention to Ryan he asks, "What happened? The last thing I remember is talking to father in the study."

"You were drugged and you're in the hospital Edward but you're going to be OK," replied Cat gently.

Looking directly into the blue eyes of his brother, he asked, "Father?"

"Yes Edward. Father."

Trying to struggle up in bed he asks, "Where is he?"

Reaching over and taking Ryan's hand, Cat quietly says, "Edward, I think there is some things that your brother needs to tell you."

Leaving the two brothers alone, Cat goes to wait outside the door.

While she waited she called Jeff to let him know that Edward was awake and at least talking and that she had left Ryan to explain everything to his brother. Their phone call was abruptly interrupted as two of the attending doctors entered the room as Ryan walked out with tears streaming down his face

"I've got to go," exclaimed Cat as she quickly ended the call.

"Ryan? What's happened?"

"He knew Cat. He knew all the time."

"What did he know? You're not making any sense."

"He knew about Lillian and me. He knew that Marion wasn't his child and he never said anything."

"But why? You're telling me he purposely let everyone believe he was responsible for his wife either leaving him or worse yet killing her?"

"He says it was guilt and he felt like he deserved to be punished for not standing up to father and refusing to marry Lillian. His guilt over marrying Lillian and depriving her of a chance of finding true happiness with someone that loved her and not just her money is what kept him silent. Worse yet, he thought that I may have had something to do with her disappearance and Boston's death. The night Lillian disappeared I had gone off to the pub but not before telling her I had changed my mind. That I really didn't love her. It was all a game with me of besting my big brother. When I woke up late the morning after Lillian disappeared I thought she had just disappeared to start a new life after our argument . Then when she failed to send for Marian and then Boston was found I feared that my cruel treatment of her had driven her to take her own life. Neither of us ever suspected father."

"Why would you? As far as you knew, he was an invalid confined to a wheelchair. Well, at least explains the strained relationship between the two of you and his lack of fatherly concern for Marion," replied Cat.

"He'd like to talk to you as soon as the doctors come out."

It wasn't long before the doctors finished their examination and brought the good news to Cat and Ryan.

The older of the two doctors said, "All his vital signs are back to normal but there does seem to be a loss of movement in one of his legs. Now, don't be alarmed. This happens quite frequently. We think that this may just be temporary and with some physical therapy he should be back to his normal self."

Breathing a sigh of relief, Ryan reached out and shaking the doctor's hand asked, "When can I take my brother home?"

"I would think tomorrow afternoon. If you leave your contact details with the ward nurse she'll phone you when he is ready to be discharged," replied the doctor.

Cat quickly thanked the doctors for everything they had done and pushed open Edward's door to find him sitting up in bed.

"How are you feeling?" asked Cat taking his hands in hers.

As he raised his eyes to meet hers he replied, "Frankly Cat. I'm still a bit confused but at least some things make better sense now and maybe Ryan and I can begin to rebuild our relationship. I'm glad he has you."

"Me? You think there's something between Ryan and me? Don't get me wrong, I think Ryan has changed and the recent events will make a much better man of him but he really isn't my type at all."

Before he had a chance to ask her exactly what her type was, a voice from the hallway jokingly yelled, "Is everyone decent in there? May I come in?"

Cat burst out laughing at the sound of Jeff's teasing voice and replied, "Barely, but come on in."

Looking around Edward asked, "Where's The O'Brien? I need to thank him for saving Cat and leading you to me in time. If it wasn't for him we could have both died."

Putting his hand on Edward's shoulder Jeff replied with fake seriousness, "In case you hadn't noticed, he's a bit too big to sneak into the hospital but he is out on the grounds with Ryan. If you just look out that window beside you then he should be able to see you. I don't mind telling you I think you've made a friend for life and I could tell he was worried about you. So as soon as Cat called and told me that you were awake I brought him along to see you."

Tapping on the window pane to get The O'Brien's attention, Jeff and Cat gently helped Edward lean sideways toward the window so O'Brien could see him.

As soon as The O'Brien caught sight of Edward, he began barking loudly and prancing around in excitement.

"And a better friend a man couldn't have. My mother used to say that the only thing that will love you more than themselves is a dog. Well, as soon as I'm discharged I'll be by to tell him a proper thank you," smiled Edward as he waved out the window to his brother and The O'Brien.

"According to Ryan that could be tomorrow and just in time to have a visit with me before I leave to head back home," remarked Jeff.

"Leaving so soon? I feel like we've just really gotten to know each other," replied Edward.

"Well, I do have to get back to my law practice. Apparently, there are way too many innocent people going to jail without the benefit of me being there to defend them," joked Jeff.

"You will come back soon, won't you?"

"Absolutely, I have to keep an eye on my tenant here. We don't want her getting into any more trouble, do we?"

Both men laughed as Cat gathered her purse to leave. "Come on Jeff, if Edward is going to get the all clear to leave tomorrow let him get some rest."

Waving goodbye at the door, the two friends headed outside to collect O'Brien and head home so that Jeff could make his flight reservations and start packing.

Back in Ballysea, Maureen stood watching out her front window and as Cat and Jeff with the O'Brien in tow climbed out of the car, she came running across the lane.

Out of breath she asked, "How's Edward? Is he going to make it?"

Smiling at her friend, Cat opened the door and said, "Yes, he's going to be fine. Come on in and I'll fill you in. I don't know about you, but I am dying for a strong coffee and a cigarette."

Maureen sat quietly sipping her coffee and taking deep drags off the cigarette as Cat told her about the conversations between the two brothers and the doctors' prognosis for Edward's recovery.

194

Finally, grinding her cigarette out in the ashtray Maureen replied, "I don't know how I could have thought Edward was capable of harming Lillian or her little dog. I am so ashamed. I let my anger over ancient history cloud my judgement."

After booking his flight back to the States Jeff rejoined the two friends.

"So you'll be leaving us?" asked Maureen.

"Yes, I'm afraid so. I have to get back to work but I leave here feeling much more comfortable about leaving Cat and The O'Brien. She's made some very good friends here that I'm sure will look after her and keep her out of mischief," replied Jeff as he pats Maureen's hand.

As Jeff leaves to begin packing, Cat walks her friend to the door and the two women with The O'Brien in the middle stand watching the sun set across the bay.

"I never get tired of this view," said Cat gazing at her friend.

"Me either. I've been watching it all my life and it grows more beautiful every night."

Suddenly remembering Jeff's last remarks, Cat throws her head back and laughing stoops down to wrap her arms around The O'Brien. "Stay out of mischief? Now, where's the excitement in that my dear friends?"

Epilogue

The following week was a very busy one as Jeff prepared to return home to Annapolis and Edward and Ryan arranged for the funerals of Lillian and their father.

The two brothers planned to run the estate as equal partners and agreed to keep the secret of Marian's true parentage between them and share the responsibility of raising Lillian's child.

In the weeks that followed, Edward regained the ability to walk without his cane and he and Cat's friendship continued to grow.

It seemed the shroud of evil that had enveloped the manor and all that lived there had finally been lifted and the village of Ballysea had returned to the idyllic Irish village of Cat's dreams.

At least, maybe for the moment...